Mention
the Night

for Graham Caveney

Don't Mention the Night

Nick Drake in 1974
Kevin Coyne in 1978
Gaffa in 2022

a memoir

David Belbin

Don't Mention the Night
David Belbin

Published in 2022 by Five Leaves Publications
14a Long Row, Nottingham NG1 2DH
www.fiveleaves.co.uk
www.fiveleavesbookshop. co.uk

ISBN: 978-1-910170-96-0

Copyright © David Belbin 2022

Printed in Great Britain

Nick Drake in 1974

People who try to analyse her brother, Gabrielle Drake wrote, "in an attempt to anchor him to their world, have nearly always exposed more about themselves than they have about their subject."

You have been warned.

I became a fan of Nick Drake in 1974, when the singer was still alive. 'Fan' is a problematic word, one I only tend to use in regard to music. Its fuller form, *fanatic*, has come to denote political or religious extremism. To me, fandom is an innocent, unalloyed pleasure. 'Fan' doesn't denote uncritical support so much as enthusiasm. Fellow fans share minutiae likely to bore non-believers silly: B sides, dropped verses, who supported who on what tour, and other trivia.

This is the story of a young Nick Drake fan, rather than the story of Drake himself. For those unfamiliar with Drake's life, however, I'll thread the key aspects through this brief memoir.

I come from a family of fans. My dad played jazz guitar. He used to carry round Big Bill Broonzy's gear for him when Broonzy had a gig in Sheffield. My mum would hang around the stage door at the City Hall to get Dickie Valentine's autograph. Dad used to claim he married Mum because her parents had bought her a terrific stereogram and he wanted to always be able to play his records on it. I suspect her being pregnant with me had rather more to do with the matter. That stereogram ended up in my bedroom, and I first heard Nick Drake through its speakers.

Nick was born in Burma in 1948 and brought up, with his sister, Gabrielle, by their parents Molly and Rodney in Far Leys, a big house in the Warwickshire village of Tanworth-in-Arden. Their mother played piano. Molly wrote and performed songs in an English folk tradition. Many of these were released after her death, at which point their influence on her son's work became clear. Nick went to Marlborough College then Fitzwilliam College, Cambridge, to study English Literature. He released three albums in his lifetime and there have been three posthumous sets, of which *Made to Love Magic* includes everything important.

I was born ten years after Nick Drake, in Sheffield. My family lived there for my first two years and in Leicester for the next three, but if a place can be said to form a person, mine was West Kirby on The Wirral, near Liverpool, where we moved when I was five. 'Please, Please Me' was number one when we arrived. I loved the Beatles. In the eleven years we lived there, my musical tastes expanded eclectically, taking in both Tamla Motown and Led Zeppelin by the time I was thirteen. For my fourteenth birthday I got tickets to my first gig, Pink Floyd playing an early version of *Dark Side of the Moon*. My taste for prog rock was superceded by a passion for singer/songwriters: James Taylor, then Joni Mitchell and Carole King; later, Leonard Cohen, Jackson Browne. Throughout, Bob Dylan.

A top of the class, imaginative kid who could draw others into his fantasy life, I got on well at primary school. Then, at eleven, I went to an all-boys grammar school where, as a speccy, borderline nerdy kid unused to having to fit in to earn others' approval, I was bullied in numerous ways. I could fight back or run from the physical bullies. Not so easy to deal with the bullies who masqueraded as friends, or, at least, peers, who resented that I was in the top stream and could talk to girls. Their bullying was more the kind that, when I became a teacher, I would see in adolescent girls: cruel teasing, threats, exclusion from the cool group. I was a weedy, constantly daydreaming youth, too naïve to hide my cleverness and flood of new opinions, hair creeping over my shoulders, proud to proclaim myself a hippy in a town where freak culture had no currency.

By the time I was sixteen, the bullying was behind me. I had a girlfriend. I wrote lyrics and poetry. The problem was my dad, who had a new job. We were only staying in West Kirby because I had to finish my O-levels, which I managed to mess up anyway.

In July 1974, we moved to the outskirts of Colne, in Lancashire, the place where my younger siblings grew up and where my dad still lived until recently. Twenty-first century Colne's fairly smart, as former mill towns go, but in the mid-'70s, the area felt run down, bleak. The housing was the cheapest in England. Nicholas Saunders' hippy bible *The Alternative Guide to England and Wales* listed Colne as the cheapest place to move to if you wanted to drop out. Lots of freaks did. It only took me a few months to meet them.

Dad had found my younger brother and me a Catholic school in Burnley, where he worked. It was meant to have the best sixth form in the area. I'd stopped attending church when I was fourteen. On my journey to atheism, I'd reached the agnostic stop. Mum and Dad said that St Theodore's got

9

great exam results and I'd need those if I was going to study Law at university. This, despite the poor O-levels, was my plan. I'd read lots of novels by Henry Cecil, felt strongly about social justice and intended to be a barrister. I agreed to go to St Theodore's High School.

Dad gave us a lift to school but we had to make the nine-mile journey home alone, changing buses in Nelson. There, I'd visit Les's Electron shop on the main road. Les sold second-hand records. I still own several that I bought there. One afternoon I picked up a 12" that had a white label and no cover, just a plain inner sleeve. One side had a blank label. On the other was written "Claire Hamill/Sutherland Bros." I'd heard of Hamill and thought I might like her. There was one song by the Sutherland Brothers I liked. The record cost 50p. It was worth a risk.

At home I plonked the disc on the stereogram that I'd recently inherited. On moving to Colne, Mum and Dad had treated themselves to hi-fi separates. The stereogram was the size of a sideboard and dominated my small bedroom at the front of the house. I put on the white label, the side with the handwriting. Two songs by each artist. Each turned out to be derivative and dull. There were four tracks on each side. I turned the disc over, expecting more of the same.

An acoustic guitar played in an open tuning over which a breathy voice began to sing about a pink moon. The guitar sound was crisp, unique, as was the voice. I was captured. The place of a middle eight was taken by a haunting – or haunted – piano solo. The whole was barely two minutes long. The next song began: "please beware of them that stare". I was captured by the wordplay, intrigued by the lyrics, which were enigmatic, brooding, and suggested some secret, shared wisdom. Who was singing? I had no idea, but I was his devotee.

The second side finished with two numbers I already knew, by Procol Harum. They were orchestrated live songs, from a record released two years before. So I could identify three-quarters of the songs on the white label, but not the ones that mattered. I played them again and again. It took weeks of detective work to figure out who they were by. I managed it with the help of an Island records catalogue provided by Les, who'd sold me the record in the first place. The singer was Nick Drake and the album was called *Pink Moon*.

The following month, I went to London for the first time, on a school trip. I didn't see the sights, except in passing. I hit the record shops. Just off Charing Cross Road I bought a copy of Neil Young's *Everybody Knows This is Nowhere* from a second-hand shop. I asked the young guy behind the counter whether he had anything by Nick Drake. 'No,' he told me, then added, 'but I admire your taste.' Nearby, at Dobell's famous record shop, I found one Nick Drake LP. It wasn't the one I was most interested in. *Bryter Layter* had a clumsy title and a poorly-designed sleeve. It wasn't cheap either, but I had to have it.

This record sounded sunnier than I'd expected, with the singer's voice lower in the mix. A couple of instrumentals had a muzaky quality. The backing singers on the track 'Poor Boy' sounded out of place to me. But there were also plenty of songs that hit me in the same spot as the two from

Pink Moon. 'Northern Sky', 'At the Chime of a City Clock' and the two 'Hazey Jane's. Most of these songs were breezier and more whimsical than the two I'd first heard, although there was dread on 'Fly' and the self-mockery on 'Poor Boy' couldn't disguise the self-pity that was also suggested by the title. The singer found it hard to express himself outside his art. "If songs were lines in conversation/The situation would be fine." Often crippled by self-consciousness, I could relate to those words.

I was an avid reader of the music papers. A few weeks later, in early December, I found, for the first time, a story about Nick Drake. He had just died, aged twenty-six, after taking an overdose of anti-depressants. That lunchtime, I made the fifteen-minute walk to Hall Street in Burnley and the original branch of Electron, run by Les's dad, Jim. I ordered a copy of the album that I knew I had to have, the one I already knew two songs from – Drake's final album, released in February 1972 – *Pink Moon*.

Two days later, I collected it. The cover was an effective Surrealist pastiche, with suggestions of Dali and Magritte, more interesting than the relatively formal cover of *Bryter Layter*. Inside its gatefold was a big photo of Drake, but it was a negative, foreshadowing the album's theme. When I got home I found that the LP, that one short piano section aside, consisted entirely of Drake singing over open tunings. The production was minimal, but vivid. The light voice was

upfront, whispering in my ear. The songs felt like they came from a darkened room.

Pink Moon is Drake's shortest and most orphic album. For those it touches, it touches them in a profound, intense way. The album is twenty-eight minutes long. Those days, I used to ration how often I played new albums, in order not to grow tired of them. But I played *Pink Moon* most days that winter, sometimes more than once a day, and I've yet to grow tired of it. The songs take you to a deep place, yet, like their singer, never fully reveal themselves.

The narrator of *Pink Moon* is defiantly naïve, while also affecting to be agelessly wise. If this is a pose, it's a convincing one. The LP's by no means a suicide note, as many have suggested. How could work of such beauty be read that way? The track whose lyric obsessed me most turned out to be called 'Things Behind the Sun'. Later I discovered that it had been written long before the rest of the album.

Pink Moon is far from life-affirming. If any message emerges from the whole, it's one of resignation, of rueful acceptance that life is meaningless and we are all isolated, unknowable. *Pink Moon*'s the only record that's ever made me cry, that first day I listened to it, but I don't know to what extent I was shedding tears for Nick Drake, dead of an overdose two and a half weeks earlier, or for myself, far from my old friends, carrying a torch for the girlfriend I'd left behind, finding it hard to relate to many of my peers in my new school.

In Merseyside I'd been active in Friends of the Earth and ran 'plant a tree in 73' at my school, giving out hundreds of tiny saplings, most of which, I hope, are by now tall, old trees. In Colne, still interested in social justice, I joined the Young Liberals. We were, essentially, anarchists. Our biggest idea was abolishing money. I found a part-time job in the warehouse at ASDA and – until they made loads of us redundant just before Christmas – earned enough money to go out drinking with a gang of older boys from the Upper Sixth. I wrote lyrics for their band. I didn't have a serious girlfriend during sixth form, partly because I tended to hang out with people older than me, and the girls I liked fancied guys older than them, not a year younger. Truth be told, I wasn't ready for a relationship. I could be silly and playful but was also intense, obsessive about music and didn't disguise my intellectual leanings, which scared off most girls I liked who might like me. I was waiting to get to university where, I hoped, I'd meet my real peers.

Twice I went back to West Kirby on my own. I saw Pink Floyd again during what turned out to be the week of Nick Drake's death. Virtually their entire set consisted of songs inspired by their founder, Syd Barrett, an acid casualty who I'd been a massive fan of for a couple of years. By the time he left the band, early in 1968, he'd come to find performing on stage impossible. Nick Drake also found live performance excruciatingly difficult. He only played about forty gigs for paying audiences, the last probably at Les Cousins on August 1st, 1970. Opening for Ralph McTell in Surrey two months earlier, he began with 'Fruit Tree', but walked off stage without completing the song. He had no stagemanship, never introducing his songs. The late Michael Chapman once told me how his wife Andru found Nick standing outside the pub after they'd been to see him at a folk club in Hull. Nick had nowhere to go so they took him home. They smoked some dope, chatted a little. When Michael got up in the morning, Nick had already left. This was, by most accounts, typical behaviour.

In 1974, changing trains in Liverpool, I visited Virgin Records on Bold St, near the station, where I bought *The Songs of Leonard Cohen*. On the way out, I bumped into Ric, a hippy entrepreneur who'd befriended fifteen-year-old me when I was involved with Friends of the Earth. I told him where I was living. Ric insisted I visit the Somewhere Community Trust in Colne. He reckoned I'd meet interesting people there. He even knew the address.

Back in Colne, I found a tumbledown pair of terraced houses at the bottom of a steep hill, surrounded by other near-derelict homes. I knocked. A bearded guy called 'Horse' invited me in. I came to know a lot of people who lived in or passed through those two, knocked through terraces, some only a year or two older than me. It was a place to which many of the young hippies who showed up in Colne gravitated. My first friend there was Neil, who had round NHS glasses and long, lanky hair. Early in 1975, we went to the Colne Municipal Hall. Singer/songwriter Tim Hardin was living in the UK at the time because he could get the heroin he was addicted to on prescription. He played a memorable show. Afterwards, Neil gave me a bit of grass as a thank you. That was the first time I smoked dope.

Nick Drake was a huge dope smoker. His first album, a copy of which I would be given that Christmas to complete my

collection, was named *Five Leaves Left*, after the slip you reached in a packet of Rizlas when the papers were about to run out. You needed four Rizlas to roll a decent joint. The publisher of the book you're reading, a Nick Drake fan, named his firm (and, later, his bookshop) after the LP's title, not realising (he claims) its stoner connection.

Less intense than *Pink Moon*, less varied and more consistent than *Bryter Layter*, with wonderful arrangements, mainly by Robert Kirby, *Five Leaves Left* is many people's favourite Nick Drake album. You can argue that some of its songs are naïve and self-consciously literary, but that's to judge it on English Literature terms. For a rock album, the lyrics are astonishingly mature. It also has a classy, green cover, on which Drake, a university student when he recorded it, looks more like a sixth-former.

By Upper Sixth, I spent all my time hanging out with the Colne hippies rather than people from my school year, none of whom lived nearby. The routine, at the sort of parties where I ended up, was that the dopers sat in a circle, smoking. There was seldom much conversation. Smoking dope tended to amplify my adolescent self-consciousness, which was already epic. Many people learn to avoid the drug because it makes them feel paranoid. I was more than satisfied to get stoned and listen to music with that foggy, free floating sensation of a journey into inner space. Being stoned also made it easier to put things into perspective.

The dope we were smoking was nowhere near as strong as the strains of weed most common today. Dope wasn't addictive (except psychologically), though I knew people who developed a tobacco habit through smoking it. Cannabis is bad for the memory. Later, I had enough sense to cut right down when I was taking my A-levels and studying for my finals.

Nick Drake discovered cannabis a year or two before he went to Cambridge and would 'self-medicate' with it for the rest of his life. The main risk of smoking dope, we were told, was that it was a 'gateway' drug. For some, it was. I tried acid a few times, as Drake may have done at around the same age (late teens), but didn't see it as a recreational drug. Rather, it was part of a spiritual quest, the same one that had us reading Carlos Castaneda, Jack Kerouac and books about Buddhism. The acid of those days, in contrast to the dope, was five times stronger than today's: too powerful to mess with. After my strongest trip, when I was eighteen, I stayed up for two days, exhilarated and, if you like, high on life.

Drake was a serious stoner. It seems likely that his prodigious cannabis intake exacerbated his depression. Research suggests that dope smokers are several times more likely to develop schizophrenia, which, in the early '70s, was the most common term for Nick's form of depression. Later, I had friends diagnosed with what was described as schizophrenia and recognised that I'd shared some of their symptoms, as so many people do, but never to a disabling extent.

There's a recording (search *Nick Drake monologue* on YouTube) of Nick rambling into a tape recorder in the early morning, having been up all night. It's the sound of a posh public-school boy who is stoned and happy. This Nick Drake had been a house captain at Marlborough and was a lethal croquet player. He taught himself guitar, formed bands and, before starting at Cambridge, travelled to Morocco, where he sang a few songs in front of the Rolling Stones, who he happened upon while visiting Tangier in March 1967.

At Cambridge, Drake was popular. He went to weekend parties in big houses and made titled friends. But he always put his music before his academic studies. *Five Leaves Left* was released to decent reviews but negligible sales. Nobody could blame Nick for pursuing a career in music rather than taking his final year. He'd just released a minor masterpiece, after all. The song 'Fruit Tree', suggesting that fame will only come long after death, would turn out to be prescient.

In 1969, Drake's words about people only knowing who you were after you're gone were a romantic notion rather than a premonition. Nick thought his work would be recognised and he expected to be famous. Even so, for the rest of his life he felt guilty about dropping out. It didn't help that, within two years, it had become clear that his musical career wasn't to be straightforward. Nick knew his records hadn't been promoted sufficiently. In 1970, his biggest supporter, Joe Boyd, sold his production company and returned to America to work on film soundtracks for Warner Brothers. Nick's final album, *Pink Moon*, was recorded over two nights in October 1971, with only engineer John Wood present. The stark, short, album, Drake's masterpiece, reached very few listeners when it came out in 1972. In total, Drake's three LPs sold only four thousand copies during his lifetime.

The 1970s were a rude awakening to many people who thought that the '60s magic would last forever. In 1971, Nick began to suffer from a depressive illness and moved back in with his parents in Warwickshire. By the time he made his final recordings, in 1974, he was no longer capable of singing and playing guitar at the same time, recording each separately. The diary his dad kept (transcribed in Gabrielle Drake's 2014 biographical compendium *Remembered for a While*) details Nick's state during those last three years in sad, repetitive detail: he went on long, aimless drives and ran out of petrol, he didn't keep himself clean, he disappeared for days on end. There were lucid periods too: the diary dismisses myths about Drake that developed over the years. For instance, it was often said that, back then, nobody knew how to deal with his kind of depression. Rodney's diaries show the support Nick received from family, friends and various doctors. While we will never know whether he meant to kill himself that November night, Nick had already taken a deliberate overdose in February of that year. His death did not surprise those close to him.

A few months after Drake's death, I began to have my writing published. There was a thriving zine culture in the mid-'70s. You'd hear about little magazines in other magazines (*fanzines* we called them then). I sent *The Hot Flash*, from Manchester, a review of the Tim Hardin concert I'd been to, which they printed. Some hippies I knew occasionally put out a magazine called *Albert*. They published two of my poems. I began to subscribe to the long established music zine *Zig Zag* and ordered the back issue including Conor McKnight's article asking 'What Happened to Nick Drake?'

It was in *Zig Zag* that I read about a new magazine out of Nottingham, *Liquorice*. Richard Thompson, whose music I'd just discovered, appeared on the cover of the first issue. I subscribed. The second issue included a new series called *Close to Your Heart*. Contributors wrote about their favourite albums. I sent them an article about *Pink Moon*. To my delight, Malcolm Heyhoe, the editor who wrote back, had not only seen and liked my Tim Hardin review but also loved Nick Drake. The magazine printed my piece over a full page in issue three.

I began to correspond with Malc at the flat he shared with his wife, Irena, in Nottingham's Victoria Centre. The University of Nottingham had a highly-rated law degree, but

Paul and I were in the middle of laying out LIQUORICE with periodic assistance from Irena. I got up and fumbled for the post, Irena's still sleeping(!). There were two very nice letters , Jim Capaldi's single and an article on Nick Drake's "Pink Moon" for our "Close To Your Heart" series. We were really pleased, a first contribution to "Close To Your Heart". and it's about Nick Drake too. "Pink Moon" is a lovely LP, time to play its' haunting tunes again. Nick Drake hung on the clouds, the sun smiled occasionally, and one day time's river flowed swiftly out of view. There aren't that many real people making real music, Nick Drake was(is) one of them. It's a pleasure to have Nick Drake:Close To Your Heart.

It's not often that you hear two songs by an artist whom you've never heard before and are so impressed by them as to want to rush out and by all the singer's LPs as quickly as possible, but it happened to me in October last year when a white label Island sampler that I picked up for ten bob in a second-hand store yielded two songs so beautiful tat I dug out an old Island catalogue to work out that the tracks were "Things Behind the Sun" and "Pink Moon" from the LP of the same name by a guy who I'd previously only heard of fleetingly called Nick Drake.

A couple of weeks later I went round practically every record store in the centre of London to find just one with a Nick Drake LP in stock, the stunningly beautiful "Bryter Lyter". I tried every possible source to get information about Nick and eventually a friend sent me a photostat of Connor McKnight's excellent article in ZigZag 42 shortly afterwards a beautiful obituary in "Sounds" by Jerry Gilbert came as a bombshell-- Nick had died from an accidental overdose of tranquilisers at 6a.m on October 26. Words can't describe how the tragedy upset me and this isn't the place for the full story (it can be found in ZZs 42 & 49) but let it suffice to say that my copy of "Pink Moon" arrived two days later and it is the only record that has ever made me cry

In the Autumn of 1971 Nick returned from a year in which he had been totally absent from the 'music scene' to record this LP. Gone were the beautiful elaborate arrangements of his first two LPs. Nick is the only person playing on the LP-- just him singing with his accoustic guitar (and piano on the title track). The only other person present at the sessions was his good friend (and brilliant engineer) John Wood. Everything that Nick recorded in on those sessions is on the LP.

The first track is "Pink Moon" and has just five lines. "Saw it written and I saw it say/ Pink Moon is on its way/ None of you will stand so tall/ Pink Moon gonna get ye all/ And its a Pink Moon.", sung twice against the guitar with a beautiful piano link Then there is "Place To Be" a sad (as are all the songs on the LP- by all accounts Nick was in a very depressed stage of his life from 1970 until a short while before he died) song about life, love, loneliness and searching...... ..for a place to be. "Road" is dominated by very strong guitar, a four line song the last two lines of which are repeated, once again, the search for a way to survive:

"You can take the road that takes you to the stars now, I can take a road that'll see me through".

"Which Will" is a loving song to the girl who has rejected him ("Which way will you take now"/if you won't take me?") It is followed by "Horn", a brief instrumental that leads into "Things Behind the Sun", which, for what it's worth, probably means more to me than any other song I know. More so than any other song on the album it is a piece of advice, the lessons that Nick has learnt realised in the song:

"Please beware of them that stare/ they only smile to see you while your time away.... ....You'll find renown where people frown/ At things that you say/ But say what you'll say" It is the longest track, the beautiful introduction breaks into the night like an anthem, it's obviously very hard for me to express the wonders of this album.

Side two opens with "Know", a short scaring song, "Know that I love you/ Know that I don't care/ Know that I see you/ Know that I'm not there". "Parasite" is another moving song in which Nick tries to put himself down but ends up impressing me of his humility. "Free Ride" can be compared to "Know" in that it has a strong rhythm and is an expression of paranoia that sets the two songs aside from the togetherness of the rest of the album. "Harvest Breed" is a short song about, I think, reaching the depths of introspection/depression-- but the ending is optimistic (again, to me) "And you're ready now for the Harvest breed" The final song is, fittingly "From the Morning". (And at this point, a big round of applause t my favourite label, Island, both for supporting Nick by putting out his albums when no-one was interested in him, and for so carefully structuring the running order of this LP that it fits together perfectly.) Perhaps I've talked too much about each song on this album but let me say tha for a man who is so obviously close to suicide, it is a warm and optimistic close.

So there you are the LP on lasts about 29 minutes but that doesn't matter to me- each song is a gem and the record is so intense and moving that time ceases to exist for me when it s playing, it seems to be over in no time at all. The songs on the LP are like epigrams which, taken as a whole, display all that th artist has learnt in his life-- songs which transcend life and death, the songs of a wise and humble man.

Perhaps this article has seemed to be a little melodrama to you; if so I don't apologise because that's what it means t me and that's what the series about. The effect that "Pink M has on me is consistent-- I ca play it three times in a row without once losing it. Someone once called the LP "an album o 3a.m. introspection" which is close but too simplistic-- lik Leonard Cohen's first three L it fills you with an air of seriousness, but the beauty of Nick's voice, guitar and songs give much more, the lyrics are so important and the emotion i so intense.

In closing, I know that most of us can't afford to for out three quid on one guy's ta but if you ever get the chance to hear Nick Drake, please try The LP of Nick's that I haven't previously mentioned a his first "Five Leaves Left" is excellent. The lyrics that have quoted ought to be credit to Warlock Music, with thanks,

DAVE BELBIN.

if it hadn't been for *Liquorice*, I'd never have put the city as my joint first-choice university. When I came over to take a test and have an interview, I visited the couple. We smoked a spliff, talking all the while about music. It turned out that smoking dope needn't get in the way of conversation when you have enough to say.

Seven mediocre O-levels was something I had in common with Drake, who went on to mess up his A-levels. He retook his at a crammer. I retook Latin in the sixth form. Nottingham was the only university to make me an offer. I owe it to Nick Drake, therefore, that I came to the city where I still live.

That autumn of '76, I spent rather more time in the Victoria Centre flats than I did on my Law course. I was invited to be an editor of *Liquorice* and nearly got to interview Jackson Browne, whose new album *The Pretender* I loved and would later name my best novel after. Neither of these were things that, at eighteen, I was ready to do. Unable to fully commit to either editing the magazine or a degree course, I managed to mess up both. That December, I dropped out, but not before securing a place on another degree course. I interviewed badly, but my A-level results and enthusiasm for the works of Bob Dylan saw me through.

I took an impromptu gap year, during which I worked on a country park, where my co-workers were mostly Colne hippies, some of whom taught me to pick magic mushrooms. That August I hitch-hiked around Europe. When I returned to Nottingham to begin a degree in English Literature and American Studies, *Liquorice* was over. I became heavily involved with the student union paper, *Gongster*. For *Gongster*, in early 1978, I interviewed John Martyn, who I'd met during my first term, backstage at a benefit concert for *Liquorice*. That night, I'd watched him snort heroin and we'd ended up in an accidental staring contest. The tough Glaswegian was thought to have been Nick Drake's closest friend in the music community (though some people dispute this). He'd even been to visit Nick at Far Leys, at the urging of Nick's parents (a 'very charming and cheerful young man with a guitar,' Nick's father wrote).

In an interview broadcast thirty years later, John recalled "He was really, really withdrawn, he found it difficult to speak. And I said, 'Listen, what the hell's gone wrong with you. Did you think you were going to be a star overnight?' And he said, 'Yes, I fucking did.'"

John only gave me the 1978 interview because I'd brought a couple of joints along ("What is it?" "Double Zero." "Ach, that's just Moroccan."). I suspect he didn't carry at the time because he was afraid of being busted. Despite this, he was happy to talk frankly about how he used drugs. These included, when he was unhappy, heroin. My interview with him, which can be found by searching the *Big Muff* website, continued with my attempt to ask him about Nick Drake. Three years after Drake's death, there'd just been an article in *The London Magazine*, touting the literary qualities of Drake's lyrics. When I mentioned this, John's manner became aggressive.

> Listen, I don't give a shit about that. I really don't wanna... I'm honestly fed up of the fucking miasma of death as

regards rock'n'roll; it just really pisses me off... Nick Drake was a very sad man; he was very, very talented, and very sad. He was a friend of mine, that's all I can tell you... I'm continually asked questions, and what happens is, precious memories are in danger of becoming anecdotes and I fucking don't want that to happen, and I think it's intrusive.

"I've turned down four interviews about Nick in the last three months, which is just great for Nick, right? But it fucking doesn't do him any fucking good now. When he was alive and kicking, no cunt wanted to know about him, nobody wanted to listen to his music, nobody played it on the fucking radio. Soon as he died all the fucking little pseudo-intellectual ponces come creeping out of their garrets in Hampstead and all the rest of it, trying to get hold of his fucking ethos, falling in love with the 'poor boy' image; it's almost slightly punk, it's so sad, it's so sad; and it wasn't affected, it was the real thing. People don't like it; people don't fucking like it; I really find the interest in him after his death disappointing and rather sickening, frankly.

We said 'fucking' a lot in those days. Even so, his anger was abundantly evident. After the show, the girlfriend I'd gone with gasped when she heard the exchange on tape, telling me how unfair he'd been. Taken aback, I'd moved the conversation on, never recovering our previously warm rapport. John continued his rock'n'roll lifestyle and I saw him play many more shows, rarely sober. He died in 2009, aged sixty.

My first term at university, exhilarated to have escaped Colne, I had crashed and burned. I did something similar at the end of my second first year, by which time I was the editor of the student union paper, which soon felt like too big a responsibility. I stood down at the start of my second year. That summer I'd moved into a shared house where I had one close friend. It had been busted the week before I moved in and would be again while I was living there. I took a top floor room which had been painted jet black by its previous resident. Not auspicious. That autumn and early winter I had my one, longish period of real depressive illness. People in my shared house noticed I was down. One gave me some pills he'd been prescribed (he didn't say what for) but never used, to help me sleep. Aged twenty, disconnected from my studies and convinced that life was meaningless, I was certain that life's one important question was whether to commit suicide. I wrote a short note and threw the full bottle of sleeping pills into my throat. They congealed in my mouth and I spat out the clump of pills. I must have come to my senses then. As far as I can recall, I took two to help me sleep and threw away the rest.

Not long afterwards, I went home for Christmas and started to feel a bit better. When I returned, another friend in the house observed how I seemed to have got over whatever had been bringing me down. It would have been uncool for him to ask exactly why I'd seemed so depressed. Bleakness was in the air. Later that year, a Colne friend, a charismatic poet a year my senior, killed himself by jumping off the roof of a multi-storey car park. Writing about him for a little literary magazine I co-edited was the nearest I came to confronting my own suicidal impulses. That's not an essay I can ever bring myself to reread. This period was to inspire my 2012 novel *Student*, in which I loosely reset some of the things that had happened to me in the twenty-first century. To distance myself further, I made its narrator female.

When I consider all the pain I'd have caused, never mind all the love and lovely things I would have missed had I succeeded in killing myself in 1978, I'm still haunted by how close I came. I've seen how suicide severely blights the lives it leaves behind. Some families seem much more prone to suicide than others. For them, the act can become, to some extent, normalised. I am not suggesting, by the way, that Drake's manner of dying in any way influenced my half-arsed attempt to kill myself. Nor am I criticising Nick Drake. Nobody knows, as his songs tell us, how cold it grows.

Early in 1979, shortly after this period of existential angst, I met the woman who I went out with for the next few years. She cured me of my late adolescent despair. Back in 1974, Nick Drake was beyond being saved by the love of a good woman. He compartmentalised his friends so that few of them knew each other, and his relationships with women were even more opaque. While he was handsome and, by all accounts, much admired, he 'had no small talk' and might sit in silence for hours. He may have had a crush on Beverley Martyn. Nick went to stay with her and John in Hastings several times, and wrote his most unabashed love song, 'Northern Sky', while he was there with them. John's song 'Solid Air', which so perfectly captures a deep but very stoned friendship, was written at the same time, about Nick.

Neither of the women with whom Nick had sort-of relationships, the singer Linda Thompson (née Peters) and the artist Sophia Ryde, appear to have slept with him. A letter to Ryde was found by Nick's bed when he died. His parents gave the sealed letter to her at his funeral. It was not a suicide note. She spoke extensively to Drake's official biographer, Richard Morton Jack, before her death in 2021. We are, therefore, likely to find out more about their relationship when his book is published in 2023.

In 1979, a boxed set of Nick's three albums was released. *Fruit Tree* was expensive, but I managed to buy the last disc separately. This was *Pink Moon* with the addition of the final four songs Nick had recorded. They were bare bones recordings on which, again, voice and guitar were done separately. 'Hanging on a Star' is addressed to Joe Boyd and others who told him that he was going to make it big, asking why his career has been neglected 'if you deem me so high'. 'Black-Eyed Dog' is a haunted blues that personalises the old image for depression to chilling effect.

Thirty years after Nick's death, when engineer John Wood prepared another remaster, he let the tape run on after 'Black-Eyed Dog'. After a long silence, another, forgotten song began. 'Tow the Line' is, like 'Hanging on a Star', about the music business. Drake probably wrote it in 1969, as he had two of the other final recordings, but in choosing to record it in 1974, Nick suggested that he hadn't entirely given up on his career, echoing the sentiments on *Pink Moon*'s 'Road': compromise with the world was still possible. He did, don't forget, make the huge effort to record these final songs. After his death, a note was found with all the lyrics to the songs that would have been on the second side of his fourth album. They weren't recorded, so we don't know if he had set them to music.

When I first played Nick Drake to my partner, she asked me to put something else on instead. The blokes in her shared house, she told me, played Nick Drake all the time, and she was tired of him. Nick's legend, I discovered, was steadily growing. At Tanworth-in-Arden, visitors would occasionally show up at Far Leys, often having travelled great distances. Several were invited to stay the night. They were given copies of home recordings as a souvenir. Some of these found their way onto bootlegs and, eventually, official posthumous releases.

There have been two Nick Drake biographies, along with several other books and documentaries. There have been concerts celebrating his songs. In 2014, *Remembered for a While* was published. Gabrielle Drake's handsome

compendium contains memoirs, essays, letters, lyrics and photos. I pre-ordered the signed, numbered, deluxe edition which included a portfolio of photographs and a 10" record of Nick's only radio session for John Peel. When Nottingham's Rough Trade record shop opened in 2014, their first event was a launch for the book. I didn't find out about it until the week after, so I didn't get the opportunity to meet Gabrielle Drake. I used to watch the actress when she was on the gameshow *Call My Bluff*, trying to see Nick's face in hers. The book is huge and you have to lift the fancy edition carefully out of its box. I'd hardly started reading it before a friend messaged me: *are you the Dave Belbin who...?* There, reprinted across a whole page of the book (293) was the piece I'd written for Liquorice, with a date written across the bottom '1974/5?'

I read the piece for the first time in nearly forty years. The first sentence of the review was still way too long, and I'd got the date of his death wrong, repeating a mistake made by the *NME*, but the content wasn't otherwise embarrassing. And now I knew that Nick's sister and parents must have seen it, saved it, perhaps even drawn some comfort from my teenage affection and enthusiasm.

I drew comfort from Nick's songs. I don't think they fed my adolescent angst. Rather, they made me feel less alone. They told me that what I was feeling and thinking wasn't unusual. They didn't offer a panacea, like Paul Simon's 'Bridge Over Troubled Water' or Carole King's 'You've Got a Friend'. They shared his view of the world. That's the most any artist can ever do. Nick Drake put his ambitions and insecurities out there. Eventually, a huge audience connected with his sensibility. I still do, too, although there are times when I'm not enamoured of Drake's studied cool. The songs' artful vagueness and stoned obfuscations create an enigmatic quality that is very English but also, occasionally, of its time. Since the '70s, more of us have learned to speak more directly about depression, partly because there seems to be a lot more of it about. It can't be said enough: we need to look out for each other. Especially at a time when our mental health services are beyond breaking point. The music business remains as cruel as it ever was. There's no support mechanism for failed stars.

For me and for many of those born in the thirty years after the Second World War, rock music has had a deep impact on our lives, far deeper than any other art form. For some of us, it continues to do so. 'Double Negative' was the original title of this chapter when it was going to be a standalone piece in an anthology. A double negative is a rhetorical device in which negative elements combine to create a positive force. This is something that, throughout his work, Nick does. The darkness, he tells us in 'Fruit Tree', can give the brightest light.

Nick Drake remains a positive force, not because he was a doomed romantic genius but because he made great art about his struggle not to become one. He failed at life, but most lives end in failure. Nick Drake's failure, with an irony that he anticipated in song, turned into a unique form of success.

KEVIN COYNE IN 1978

In October 1976 I spent more time in the Victoria Centre flats than I did in my law lectures. My hall of residence room, meanwhile, became a ticket office. *Liquorice* was having a benefit gig to put the magazine on a more secure financial footing. Bridget St John, Kevin Coyne and John Martyn had all agreed to play the Victoria Leisure Centre, on the edge of the city, at the end of the month. I already had one album by Bridget and was a John Martyn fan, but had never heard of Kevin Coyne. His photo was on the cover of the new issue, number 7, which had a big interview with him inside. I borrowed his double album debut for Virgin, *Marjory Razor Blade*. The sound was raw, showcasing a bluesy voice with shades of Joe Cocker. Coyne's songs dealt with marginal lives and mental illness. The instrumentation and arrangements were rudimentary but effective. The song that stuck with me on first play was 'House on the Hill', a haunting, compassionate ballad about being committed to a mental asylum.

From my ground floor room at Cripps Hall of residence in the University of Nottingham, I sold over a hundred tickets for the benefit at £1.25 a pop (good value, even then). Selling the tickets provided an instant introduction to many of the more hip members of the student community, one of whom, Richard, I ended up sharing a house with the following year. On the night itself, I was on hosting and taping duties. John Martyn turned up with a solid electric guitar for the first time. I snatched a couple of minutes of him improvising in the soundcheck. Later, he would use the solid on stage for the first time, performing a new song he'd written for guitarist Paul Kossoff, who'd recently died, 'Dead on Arrival'.

LIQUORICE

music'n'allsortz

no.7 1976　　　　　　　value at 20p!

Kevin Coyne　　　　Joni Mitchell
Robert Wyatt's Diary
Soft Machine　　　& Lots More

Bridget, following a short set by Brindaband, played beautifully, despite the rowdy crowd. We'd sold out and then some. She was a huge talent and her latest album *Jumblequeen*, which she signed a copy of for me that evening, holds her strongest work. She had several outstanding new songs too. Over the coming years I listened to my recording of her set until the chrome tape wore out. Bridget played one more gig the following week, then moved to New York, where she would work as a cleaner, have a daughter and later marry Stevie Wonder's bass player. I didn't see her perform again until 2000.

Kevin Coyne (1944-2004) was a singer-songwriter, born in Derby in the East Midlands. He trained as an artist and worked as a social therapist in mental hospitals for four years. A powerful singer, with a strong interest in the blues, he teamed up with former Bonzo Dog Doo-Dah Band bassist Dave Clague. They formed Siren, who were signed by John Peel for his Dandelion label, which later released Coyne's first solo album, the remarkable *Case History*, in 1972. After their singer's sudden death, Kevin was asked to replace the deceased Jim Morrison in The Doors (the two acts were on the same label, Elektra, in the US). He said no. Kevin was Virgin Records' second signing. They asked him to add vocals to the debut of their first signing, Mike Oldfield, an album called *Tubular Bells*. Kevin said no to that, too.

Virgin Records released *Marjory Razor Blade* in 1973. The double album received a great deal of critical acclaim and remains his best-known work. Kevin put together a band that featured blues legend Zoot Money and future Police guitarist Andy Summers. They made a couple of albums and a live double but never broke big. For a more complete biography of Kevin, there's a full, accurate account on Wikipedia. There is also a wealth of material – indeed, a kind of oral history – on Pascal Regis's website *Kevin Coyne: Warts and All.*

That night in Nottingham, in the changing rooms that formed the backstage, Kevin admired my *Liquorice* T-shirt and blagged one 'for the kid'. He refused the veggie food on offer and went for beans on toast at a nearby cafe. Later, with a wink to me, he shoved another T-shirt under his arm. Kevin was mildly aggrieved that he was only getting £35 'expenses' to John Martyn's £100 (for another £100, we'd been offered Danny Thompson on bass). Small and a little rounded, while not noticeably overweight, he was an impish presence, flirting with the pretty but shy Bridget (who he knew from their days on John Peel's Dandelion label). I watched Martyn snort heroin before going onstage, but Kevin didn't even partake in the joints that were handed around. His work with the mentally ill had left him wary of mind-altering drugs.

Kevin was on after Bridget but I couldn't record his set. His act made use of backing tapes, and we needed the cassette deck for them. I'd never seen or heard anything like Kevin that night. His transformation from the mischievous man I'd met in the changing rooms reminded me of Liverpool Stadium, three years earlier, when I'd chatted to a young Japanese man on the stairs, not knowing who he was. A few minutes later Damo Suzuki was on stage, fronting the band, Can: a frantic, magnetic performance that changed the way I thought about music.

This is what I wrote about Kevin's set not long afterwards. "Playing before a Nottingham audience mostly unfamiliar with his songs, he forced open their sensibilities. The songs were (are) about loneliness and love, dreams of movie stars and the reality of fat girls, the pain of living within an often-hostile society. Kevin used uncannily disturbing backing tapes of himself and never seemed to stand still; at one point he did a dance for us, with a chair on his head; during 'Good Boy' he spat at the audience, literally. Someone called out for 'House on the Hill'. 'I'm not that playing that one,' Kevin said. 'It's about lunatics.'"

Like Damo, Kevin improvised freely on stage and had a shaman-like quality, but there the resemblance ends. Damo sang poetic nonsense, where the sound of the words was all that mattered. Kevin's words had been freely written but were always rewritten in the heat of the moment. Bob Dylan often changes phrases, even whole lines in his old songs. Kevin did the same, earlier, sometimes making up new verses or even whole numbers on the spot. His work appealed to the part of my brain that would soon, reluctantly conclude that I ought to be studying something more cerebral than the law.

The songs, even on first listen, cut deep into the human condition. The one that stuck with me most was 'Talking to No-one' ('talking to no-one is strange, talking to someone is stranger') but the whole fifty minutes were a revelation. There was plenty of humour in his performance but there was also menace, and not everyone liked it. When he sang 'Good Boy' and spat at the audience during the line 'you're just a – lick spittle', the girl next to me closed her eyes and lowered her head, a grimace of revulsion spread across her face.

Kevin was doing something serious and original with the singer/songwriter genre – not the introspection that characterised Martyn, Drake or my favourite at the time, Jackson Browne, but a scathing view of the world laced with a deep empathy for those that it left behind. This vision was fundamentally, though I didn't realise this implicitly until later, a Roman Catholic one, a background I shared with him, though I'd stopped going to church when we moved to Colne.

I lasted four weeks on the Law degree and switched briefly to Philosophy and Psychology, which turned out to be equally unsuitable to my temperament. Happily, one of the friends I'd made through selling the benefit tickets told me about a degree course that sounded more up my street. It was English Literature, with less of the old stuff that looked like a slog (although had I known that I would have to teach *Beowulf* and Wordsworth at undergraduate level thirty years later...) combined with the literature part of an American Studies degree. I secured a place for the following autumn before I quit Philosophy. So, though I dropped out, as I mentioned earlier, I did have a place to return to. I was even able to persuade my local education authority to extend my grant by one term.

From January 1977, I worked outdoors, in Wycoller Country Park, where my co-workers included a wide range of misfits and hippies. We learnt to build drystone walls and dig drains. After seven months, I'd saved enough money to finance hitching around Europe for a month. During this accidental gap year, I caught up with Kevin's back catalogue. Soon I had *Marjory Razor Blade*, *Blame it on the Night* and the live double *In Living Black and White*.

I was also amassing life experience that made me relate more closely to Kevin's work. Enough happened during those few months of 1977 to fill another memoir. I read my poetry in folk clubs. It's likely that the example of Kevin's set at the Victoria Leisure Centre had influenced and helped free something in me. Two or three times I even accompanied myself on rudimentary guitar. My main party piece was a surreal serial story called 'Captain Horizontal the Vertical Cowboy' in, I think, four parts. Just before I finished at the Country Park, a whole crew of my workmates came to watch me perform the finale at a Nelson folk night and the host was forced to fit me in even though he had a guest booked.

I made two friends who lived ten minutes' walk away in Laneshawbridge, occupying a tiny terrace by the river that ran past the bottom of our home. Fred and Delia had moved to Colne because it was cheap, then both got jobs as Conservation Rangers at Wycoller. Through them I met Kathy, a runaway from Virginia (her parents were living in the UK) who was staying with them. She'd briefly gone out with a friend of theirs and he'd hidden her with them.

Fred and Delia were happy to offload Kathy onto me several evenings a week. We watched horror movies together and she read my poetry, though romantically we didn't take things very far. I told my mum that Kathy was a year younger than me. But I knew she was only fifteen, albeit wise for her years, and my mum knew I was lying. Kathy did a runner (with my new green sweater) when her parents' private detective was on the verge of tracking her down. I don't know what happened to her after that.

I sometimes wonder whether those three or so years I spent in Colne, after middle-class West Kirby, were the deciding factor in my becoming a creative writer. I'd had the writer's temperament for as long as I can remember, but 1977 was the year that I formed the ambition which would be behind all my thinking from then on: to write novels.

1977 is remembered as the year of punk, and I bought the records, but it was also, in a sense, the end of the '60s, a time when the hippy dream that had dragged so many people to Colne and nearby villages began to pall and sour. At the time of writing, we still have a family home in Colne, and I go back there once or twice a year, but the town of those days is long gone. Most of the hippies, I presume, integrated, went straight, or moved to Wales.

That autumn, back in Nottingham, *Liquorice* was over. I still hung out with its former editors. My *Liquorice* connections secured me an import copy of the next Kevin Coyne album, a compilation called *Beautiful Extremes 1974-7*, only released in the Benelux countries, where Kevin was a bigger name. The set brought together a bunch of recordings from the last three years, melding them into a coherent, expansive whole that showed the full range of Kevin's oeuvre. It would only be released in the UK six years later, in a bastardised version, by Cherry Red.

Beautiful Extremes forms the best introduction to the full range of Kevin's work. Often the only accompaniment is Bob Ward's acoustic guitar or basic piano. The plaintive, primitive 'Something's Gone Wrong' is followed by the desperate 'Looking for the River' which is Beckettian in its

Beautiful Extremes: 1974-1977
Kevin Coyne

stark simplicity. Even better is the ballad that follows, 'Roses in your Room', a passionate love song that, by avoiding specifics, gets over Kevin's entire world view in a few lines. People hurt each other all the time. They try to control each other. The sentiment that love is never easy recurs throughout Kevin's work, but never in a clichéd way. His love songs come with a generosity of spirit, a lack of self-regard, a world away from rich, self-satisfied US singer songwriters nursing obscure grievances.

'All the Battered Babies', with its anguished vocal and distorted guitar, is a much harder listen. The verses are full of pain, the chorus a compassionate plea. The effect is heart wrenching. It closes Side A. Side B has two of Kevin's more avant-garde numbers (think Brecht musicals), 'Rainbow Curve' and the absurdist 'Mona, Where's my Trousers?' These two, along with 'Roses in Your Room' are the only tracks from the album to have been released on CD (on the now out of print four-CD Virgin anthology *I Want my Crown, 1973-1980*. 'Roses...' also features on the great one-CD Coyne anthology from 2013, *Voice of the Outsider*. It's also out of print and ruinously expensive).

Sandwiched between these more extreme numbers is Kevin's most beautiful love song, one which would be released as a single in the '80s and covered by Everything but the Girl. 'So Strange' is an affecting, arresting love song from the point of view of the outsider, backed by Bob Ward's gentle, effective strumming. I'm reminded of it when I'm walking in Nottingham's Arboretum. 'See the bandmaster on his stand, conducting the leaves.' The album's final song 'Fool, Fool, Fool' finds Kevin in self-eviscerating mood. We've all felt like that song's narrator. Both it and 'All the Battered Babies' were replaced when the album got a belated UK release in 1983, a maddening decision.

Early in 1978, Kevin released a companion collection of new songs, *Dynamite Daze*. I say 'companion collection' advisedly. Kevin told me that this was his intention. The two albums even share the same elements of cover design. I would argue that *Dynamite Daze* and its successor, *Millionaires and Teddy Bears* mark the peak of Kevin's work. A 2021 'how to buy' article in *Mojo* magazine placed *Dynamite Daze* at number one.

Dynamite Daze includes 'Lunatic', a tender ballad, and probably my least favourite track. It's too on the nose. He'd said it all better elsewhere. It's preceded by the title track, an exhilarating statement of intent, full of humour and Kevin's take on punk rock. Kevin's over thirty but he can still rock. He's in a rage, he sings, challenging the punks to come out to play. Not that there was any antipathy to him from that direction. Three years later, he would record an LP with The Ruts, while, in 1977, on the Tommy Vance show for Radio London, John Lydon (aka Johnny Rotten) played two hours of his favourite music, including one of the best songs from *Marjory Razor Blade*, 'Eastbourne Ladies', a choice that emphasised – musically and lyrically – that the punk rock stance was emerging well before anyone gave that name to it.

The beautiful 'Are We Dreaming', backed only by Paul Wickens' sublime organ part, is a secular hymn. 'I Really Live Round Here (False Friends)' is an angry riposte to neighbours who treat Kevin as some kind of stuck-up rock star. 'I'm not a millionaire and my patience is thin.' The first side has light relief in the music hall song 'Take Me Back to Dear Old Blighty'. Yet perhaps the most important song on the album is the half sung, half spoken version of John Clare's great poem, 'I Am', which was my introduction to Clare.

Twenty-five years later, I found myself giving lectures in the John Clare Lecture Theatre, a name bestowed it by my friend John Goodridge, one of the world's leading Clare scholars. Clare (1793-1864) was a labouring class poet who was taken up by the London literary establishment. He was never comfortable in that crowd but his education also separated him from his illiterate peers. Isolation and estrangement were central themes of his, as were his joy in nature and anger about the effects of the Helpston enclosure act of 1809. The enclosure acts denied commoners access to much of the countryside. Like Kevin, Clare was a small man who used drink to relax. He suffered from severe delusions and spent his last twenty-three years in Northampton General Lunatic Asylum, where he wrote 'I Am.'

> I am—yet what I am none cares or knows;
> My friends forsake me like a memory lost:
> I am the self-consumer of my woes—

"It's the Clare poem everyone knows," John Goodridge says of Kevin's version, "and of course Coyne would have especially zoomed in on the mental health issues in it, with his own complex background. Interestingly, the same year Clare wrote it, 1848, he also wrote 'Little Trotty Wagtail', his most joyously childlike lyric – the two extremes of his late consciousness." Clare's influence on Coyne is clear. 'Looking for the River', one of his most poignant songs, is a good example. Kevin once told me why he was drawn to Clare.

"The most powerful work he did was when he was incarcerated. He became a sort of star in London for a while. His books of poems sold. He was a very simple man really. I know some of his feelings for that. I can understand what happens, in a sense it's happened to me in many ways. Being in the asylum, he was totally neglected by his family as far as I can gather... I can think of no other way of encapsulating that feeling about self. That is my theory I am yet what I am. At the darkest moment who cares or knows, you have to eat your own pain really, because there's no-one else. Also, if you've an awareness of pain, in yourself, your awareness of other people's pain, for me, is acute as that."

Side two of *Dynamite Daze* begins with the single that preceded it, 'Amsterdam', one of his catchiest numbers. The heat is on down at the Melkweg (still a key Amsterdam music venue) and dope smoke is knocking the punters out. There's a good TV version of this exhilarating song to be found on YouTube (from the Dutch show *Top Pop*). Sometimes Kevin would change its 'honey' in 'Honey, honey where are you?' to 'Lesley', his wife's name. I was to get a strong sense of the loneliness of the touring musician in Manchester on March 31st, 1978.

For some reason, the *NME*, the only music weekly that counted in the late '70s, hadn't reviewed *Dynamite Daze*. Annoyed and sensing an opportunity, I typed up a review and sent it off. Deputy editor Neil Spencer did write back to me, saying Charles Shaar Murray had been meant to review the album but had had 'a bout of doubt'. A new review had already been commissioned. Extraordinary, looking back, the seriousness of the response I got, but I was a serious young man, just turned twenty and sure such attention was Coyne's due.

I was keen to see Kevin live a second time and noticed he was playing Rafters, a Manchester club, during the Easter break. I'd passed my driving test and Manchester was only an hour's drive from Colne. Moreover, I'd recently interviewed John Martyn and Roy Harper for *Gongster*. It would be great, I thought, to interview Kevin, whose phone number I was able to get through *Liquorice*. I rang, explained who I was and what I wanted to do. He said "yes."

"Are you the guy that rang earlier?" Kevin was a bit trimmer than eighteen months earlier and wore a smart leather jacket. Almost the first thing I did to establish my *bona fides* was show him the review I'd sent the *NME*, which he read with interest. "Better than Dylan, eh?" he said, with a twinkle in his eye. "Maybe that's going a bit too far." Later in the year I was to see Bob twice, at Earl's Court and Blackbushe. I was a huge fan, but one prone to exaggeration when it came to things I loved. Kevin then told me how the *NME*'s Nick Kent had visited his house the week before to do a long interview. He'd been very impressed by how clever Kent was. The interview, 'Kevin Coyne: Matching Girth and Vision!' was in the *NME* dated April 15th, 1978, along with a review of the new album by Monty Smith.

"Arguably the most disorientatingly humane, compassionate and underrated artist working within this bloated shallow medium known as 'rock' at this moment in time," wrote Kent. He, along with many others, identified 'House on the Hill' as the key Coyne song. This impassioned ballad is narrated by someone about to go into an asylum, but some listeners hear 'House on the Hill' as a song about a prison, which, in a sense, it is. Prisons are often built on hills. I can see one from my back garden.

"Punk didn't really teach me anything," Kevin told Kent. "It was just a confirmation of my principles really." Earlier that year, in *Sounds*, he said "I like Johnny Rotten's approach. I think I've been doing it all my life anyway. So what the fuck. His pain's right on view."

In Rafters' tiny dressing room, once the tape was on, we discussed his recent musical *England, England* and his next theatrical project, a romantic opera with some relation to the Moors Murderers, *Babble*. Who might sing the female part? I asked. Carole Grimes had turned it down. I suggested Bridget St John ('a class singer') or Julie Tippett. "Nah, Dagmar's the best of the painful brigade." A telling phrase.

Bob Hoskins, then starring in Dennis Potter's seminal series *Pennies From Heaven* on BBC1, had the main role in *England, England*. "Bob was magnificent, without flattening anybody, without over-acting. And he sung fucking great." Kevin told me about meeting Charlie Kray as part of his research. "Bland. Very moral." We talked about his growing up in Derby in the '50s. "It was very grey then. There wasn't a lot of money around and not a lot of hope, really."

I asked him about the opening lines of 'Dynamite Daze'. "That's an answer to Johnny Rotten. Don't tell me about age, I understand what reality is too. That goes into 'Brothers of Mine' which is in a way an attempt to mirror some of my pain, singing to the proletariat, if you like, about them and about our problems, and seeing their brainwashed, totally disinterested attitude to the things that I said are getting increasingly better all the time." He told me about John Clare and went on to give me the background to my favourite song on the new album, 'Juliet and Mark'. "I was feeling unusually optimistic. Knowing anyway that in the end you've got to let the curtains fall down and let the light shine in 'cos otherwise... that's if you want to carry on living in some recognisable shape with some optimism."

He added, "Some of the songs are very profound and I remember that, and yet, you've got to remember that most of the songs are done very spontaneously and on the spur of the moment. It follows through my feeling that I'm just an organ for whatever's out there. Sometimes it just seems to work that way. I find that with drawing too. Images just seem to come, which goes back to, say, William Blake... he had a vision. Because it has to be a vision... Occasionally I repeat things, but I don't mind that, it keeps that diaristic run through all the albums, regardless of their production or who's on them. In the end it's true to my state of mind at the time."

We disagreed on the merits of David Bowie's recent work (*Low* and *Heroes*), which Kevin had gone off, but he was enthusiastic when I said that I thought his nearest peer was Randy Newman. "I think so. Yes, I do." Turned out he'd been introduced to the recent *Little Criminals* on a Scandinavian tour and was catching up on Newman's earlier albums. He praised Newman's "wonderful sense of irony. Obviously a lover of humanity yet at the same time appalled by what they do." I put it that "practically all of Newman's songs encompass a blanket irony. There're very few where you feel that he is actually singing from the heart." "Yeah, but in a way that, to me, is the honesty of it all... that's the art in it really, the skill."

We talked about the concept of the 'singer/songwriter' who's supposed to be 'letting it all out'. "The singer/songwriter thing I've always found bewildering... I just think of myself as an explainer, a communicator. It's unfortunate though, up to now there's been no place for me, there's been no category provided."

He was still optimistic about having great success, and thought, rightly, that the new album was by far his best. "When people say 'oh, it's a shame' [that he'd not had a big success], that only happens in England...' what they're talking about basically is money. You should have a yacht. Little realising that they're all the things I despise really... but I've no doubt at all that all those things will face me at one time or another... it'll be interesting to see what happens, and it will, I think."

I asked him how he wrote songs. "I just get an idea, a line, an image, then start on the guitar and try and find a tune to fit the first words and let it all come out. Sometimes it doesn't. If it's a phoney idea, not heartfelt."

I mentioned that I was brought up as a Catholic. "I didn't know that," he said, as though he should have been able to tell. His attitude to the callow student interviewing him softened a little. "Yeah," I replied, "and I still feel the effects strongly." "You will for the rest of your life. Yeah, it is once a Catholic, always a Catholic. That's the way I feel about it. A sense of spirituality, a sense of right and wrong, light and dark, extremes if you like."

That part of the conversation has always stayed with me. A Catholic upbringing does make you look at the world in black and white. You can't be a wishy-washy agnostic. You have to choose. And it's a big break, that point when you succeed in training your brain not to believe that God is watching your every action, hearing your every thought. Catholic guilt, that nagging sense of responsibility for bad things you've done or good things you've failed to do, is harder to shake and continues to condition my behaviour, along with that of every other ex-Catholic I know.

"It's a very lush sort of religion, very rich, like meat with cream on it," Kevin went on. This led us to the last song we discussed, 'Are We Dreaming?' "That's a sort of... hymn. All those images of the large hospital with the bowling greens, the little lake with the bower. Am I in a dream? Me, sitting there in silence, in isolation, that's all really... in a sense it's just a collection of images, but it's about old age and it's about the new age and it's about hope."

We were an hour or two away from that evening's gig. "They're not ordinary gigs that I do. I have to give of my very best, every night, regardless of some of the audiences, which, fortunately, remain very good. Places like this, they don't really set a situation up with all this loud music and beer, people getting drunk."

The interview ended there. Kevin gave me a suspicious look when I turned on the tape recorder again when we were chatting afterwards, but I'm glad I took the risk, because otherwise I wouldn't have remembered his thoughts about his writing methods.

I told Kevin how Roy Harper had recently said of a line I'd praised. "That line only took me half an hour." "It's a very

George "Zoot" Money with Kevin, late '70s

short time for him whereas I feel with you it's much more spontaneous," I told Kevin. "Oh yes, spontaneity is so much of it. Those who are unable to produce quickly is for me very hard to understand. Some people find it hard to believe that you can do that – that you can sing a song one way and then change the words the next time and maybe a third time and continue and you can drop out a line. Sometimes it can be hard, you can lose some good ones."

After the interview, while the small club slowly filled, I played pool with the unassuming, approachable George, who, at the time, I knew only as Kevin's keyboard player, rather than the blues legend, 'Zoot' Money, he already was. George and I played doubles, taking on all comers, and only lost the table when George insisted we didn't carry over the two shots due us after an opponent error. "An unfair rule." George told me he prided himself on being able to follow any singer, but Kevin put him to the test.

"Beautiful Extremes?" I asked him.

"Yeah. That's it exactly."

The venue, as Kevin had suggested, was a bit of a dive. There were less than a hundred people at the gig. Yet the show was one of the great gigs of my life, a blistering, intense, occasionally furious, utterly absorbing 75 minutes. I would see Kevin many more times but never better. That gig was an unrepeatable combination of seeing an artist at the point when I'd just fully embraced their music, seeing them perform their finest work at a time when the songs were new, accompanied by the one musician who always brought out the best in them. George, with his jazz pedigree, was used to improvisation, clearly enjoyed the high wire act of figuring out what Kevin was going to do in the moment – and the one after that.

The set included most of the new album, including my favourite 'Juliet and Mark', about a couple (if they even are a couple) who are both trapped in despair, yet are brought out of their unhappiness by music. 'Funny how the gramophone always seems to play when you're up, up, up in this world.' It's the flip side of 'The World is Full of Fools' from Kevin's next album. As it ends, one character tells the other, 'I've found my spirit again.'

Kevin also sang Johnny Ray's angst-ridden 'Cry'. He and George did at least part of 'Dance of the Bourgeousie', a piss-take of the avant garde, which I saw him perform more than once. 'Amsterdam' and the new album's title track were highlights. Although there are no recordings of this night, or indeed this brief tour, there is, thankfully, a superb document of Kevin's partnership with George from the following year on German TV's *Rockpalast*. Now released as a CD/DVD package, that set also includes songs from 1979's *Millionaires and Teddy Bears*. Most of it can also be found on YouTube as individual songs.

Kevin normally limited himself to, at most, two encores, but that night he did four, including 'Marlene' with a made-up-on-the-spot extra verse. "Best fucking audience I've seen in ages," he said.

That night, as we parted, I said, "Better than Dylan, I meant it." "Nah," Kevin replied, "that was just tonight. Tomorrow night we'll be better than Dylan."

I saw Kevin again in 1978. Four of us drove to the second of the infamous *Babble* gigs at the Rock Garden. "Oh, it's the student," George said when I bumped into him beforehand. That would have been how the pair thought of me. Kevin drew in musos and oddballs but was never remotely cool or fashionable and rarely played universities or colleges. Student fans were unusual and possibly a little suspect. Kevin's music was too raw, perhaps, too visceral and demanding, lacking aspects that made him mysterious or the least bit hip.

The Rock Garden was even more of a toilet than Rafters. Kevin's rock opera was meant to feature Kevin and Dagmar

Krause, but George explained that she'd absented herself from the second night after tabloid stories attacking the first. The problem was that *Babble*'s story was supposedly inspired by the Moors Murderers, even though they aren't explicitly referred to in the rock opera. The official reason for Dagmar's absence was illness. She's on the record, so I'm glad that I got to hear Kevin perform all the songs and the spoken monologues placed between them, which aren't on the album.

For some, including Bonnie 'Prince' Billy, who has covered two of its songs and on tour performed the whole opera with Angel Olsen, *Babble* is the most important of Kevin's albums. It's a hard but satisfying listen. A recording of the first night, with Dagmar, and many others can be found on Pascal Regis's online archive of live recordings, *The World of Kevin Coyne*. It's worth hearing for Zoot's musicianship and Kevin's otherwise unavailable monologues.

I've described in the preceding essay the pit of depression I fell into in late '78, the first term of my second year. Before it set in, I set up a meeting in the Lenton pub The Three Wheatsheaves to find a new editorial team for the student union paper. Once they were installed and knew what do, I quit.

My experience of depression wasn't unusual, or even severe, compared to many. Chris, my closest friend on the small joint honours course, disappeared from university for virtually the entire second year. When he returned in the third year, visibly cheered by his new girlfriend, we never discussed why he'd been away. I never mentioned the state I'd been in either.

The music I was listening to may have been a symptom of my depression, but was hardly a cause, and I didn't change my listening habits greatly when it lifted. That January, there was a new Kevin Coyne album.

These days, the gaps that artists leave between albums often stretch to several years, but that wasn't the way in the '70s, arguably the peak of the LP as an art form in its own right. The form was to be sullied by CDs – up to twice as long – where tracks could be shuffled or skipped, and then trammelled by streaming platforms.

Yet, less than a year after *Dynamite Daze*, Kevin released *Millionaires and Teddy Bears*, his most coherent, best

produced album. It's also my favourite, probably helped by its coming out a week after my 21st birthday, when I had just started seeing Barbara, with whom I had my first serious relationship.

The whole of *Millionaires* feels like it's in full colour after the black and white of its two predecessors. The cover, one of Kevin's paintings, reflects this. It's no wonder that, in our interview, Kevin felt so optimistic about breaking through that year. He was at his absolute artistic peak.

The sound of *Millionaires* is more varied, the structure more traditional. There are no covers or avant-garde moments. The nearest to an experimental track is the opener 'Having a Party' where Kevin dreams of going to a millionaire's house with its display of gold discs and is asked where his are. He confesses that he hasn't got one, not a single gold disc at all. It's an arresting, catchy song which he would perform for the rest of his career. But it was a risk, because one of the millionaires he's singing about has to be Richard Branson, boss of Virgin, the label Kevin was signed to.

Millionaires only appeared briefly on CD, though six of its ten songs do feature on the *I Want My Crown* anthology. Among them is the gorgeous 'I'm Just a Man', a naked, very vulnerable, raw monologue that captures what it's like to love freely and honestly. Even better is 'Marigold', with its digs at a naïve radical feminist, with Randy Newman levels of irony and humour.

The album concludes with my favourite Kevin Coyne song, 'The World is Full of Fools'. It's one of his most 'written' songs. Kevin claimed never to write down his songs, even getting his sons to transcribe the words for LP lyric sheets rather than do it himself. Every performance remade the songs anew. But he rarely changed the words of 'The World...' on stage.

Over a church-like organ, the song's narrator tells us about his isolation, being trapped inside the house, unable to go out on a sunny day. A big bookcase hides the window. He's going to keep it right, he tells us, but 'don't mention the night'. The subject of night, which tends to represent Kevin's depression, recurs throughout his work. One of his best earlier albums is called *Blame it on the Night*.

The narrator of 'The World is Full of Fools' sits by the lakeside, with white squares of paper 'full of ideas' strewn all around him. He throws them into lake and watches them sail away. 'The world is full of fools,' he tells us, 'but it doesn't make them bad people.' In the second verse a friend urges him outside to go outside and enjoy the sunshine. He tries to explain why he can't. 'I know I'm deep, I seem to be asleep.' But it's not too late. The world might be full of fools 'but it doesn't make me a bad person.'

I only saw Kevin sing the song once, at Derby's Pennine Hotel in February 1979, where I said hello to him before the show. I'd grown a beard and, surrounded by people from his past, he didn't remember who I was. 'Manchester,' I said. He repeated 'Manchester', shaking his head. We parted.

I'd wanted to send him the three-page *Gongster* interview when it came out, but Malc wouldn't give me Kevin's address. He hadn't liked the way I mentioned backstage details (repeated here) from the Victoria Centre benefit and felt that I should have edited the interview rather than post a full transcript. It was a fair point but I couldn't make the time. Shorter is more work. Lucky in a way. I'm glad that, tape long lost, I still have the full transcript to draw on.

In the early '80s, Kevin's marriage to Lesley broke up. He became an alcoholic and had a nervous breakdown, partly chronicled in the albums *Bursting Bubbles* and *Sanity Stomp*. He moved to Nuremburg and slowly rebuilt a career in Germany. There are flashes of greatness in the music he made between then and his death in 2004, although I can't pretend to have followed him as closely after 1982. After a spoken word event at Nottingham's Midland Group in 1981, where there was an exhibition of Kevin's paintings, I didn't see Kevin live for several years.

He had a bit of a comeback in the late '80s, with the albums *Stumbling Onto Paradise* and *Everybody's Naked*. I saw him three more times in Nottingham and Derby, with a band, then a smaller band, then solo, the audiences smaller each time. His career was elsewhere. He made a lot of albums in his last twenty years and doubtless there are gems I've yet to mine. For me, though, the songs rarely reach the transcendent peaks he climbed in the '70s. Often Kevin fell back on the default blues and early rock'n'roll stylings with which he'd begun his career. He felt safe there.

Kevin stopped drinking in 1985. He spent more time painting and wrote three books, two published by Serpents Tail in the UK, along with operas about, amongst others, Syd Barrett. In Nuremburg he met and married Helmi and performed until his death from lung fibrosis, aged sixty. In his final months he'd have an oxygen tank on stage with him. I have a recording of his penultimate gig, given a week before his death in Halle, Germany. 'Dynamite Daze' is the penultimate number. The last words of the last song, 'My Story', are 'I love you.'

There was a tribute album. While Kevin was more fêted on the continent than at home, he had fervent admirers. I discussed him with the late, great Jackie Leven the last time he played in Derby. Jackie's song 'Here Come the Urban Ravens' describes Kevin with 'a ticket in his hand for the underground'. In 2017 a BBC blue plaque celebrating Kevin was erected outside Derby Art School, where he studied from 1961-65.

In 2019 I appeared on John Holmes' BBC Radio Nottingham radio show for his version of *Nottingham Island Discs* (a full hour with eight complete songs, but no book or luxuries) talking about my life and the songs that were important in it. I wanted to end with 'The World is Full of Fools'. But the song wasn't in the BBC's 'jukebox' library. The producer couldn't even locate it on YouTube. We made do without.

Happily, Kevin is better remembered in Germany, where he ended his days. In 2021 the first book about Kevin's work appeared, cowritten by Karl Bruckmaier and Steffen Radlmaier. Its title translates as *The Crazy World of Kevin Coyne: artist and rock poet*. It's particularly interesting on Kevin's early days, the breakdown years, and how Helmi rescued him in the '80s. In 2022, with Helmi's cooperation,

Stefan Voit launched an official, impressively comprehensive Kevin Coyne website at https://www.kevincoyne.de

Decades after his death, Nick Drake found the audience he'd thought his work deserved. Kevin's work has never found anything approaching a mass audience. Perhaps, given the work's unvarnished truthfulness, it was never likely to. Nor is it likely that Drake's back catalogue would have had the same kind of success had he not died so young.

It's hard to imagine Nick Drake making a living from playing live, as most musicians have to these days. Far more talented people are left behind than make it. The end of Bridget St John's recording career proves that. Talent and determination are prerequisites for success. Luck and vaulting ambition are also required. Nick and Kevin had little of either.

In 1978, I asked Kevin about his other favourite writers. He talked about Harold Pinter, whose influence on him was predictable, but also mentioned Philip Larkin. The poet is, in many ways, Coyne's opposite. "I think he's a little precious but writes with a lot of insight... there's a sense of terrific straining in his work." They also share, at key points, the nihilistic sense of transcendence that Larkin conveys in the closing lines of 'High Windows' – 'nothing – nowhere – endless'. For all his innate conservatism, Larkin, like Coyne, reaches into the heart of the human condition with clarity and compassion. What moves me most in Coyne's work and, more elliptically, in Drake's, is the way that – to paraphrase Larkin's 'Church Going' – listening to them feeds the hunger in ourselves to be more serious.

For atheists, art can replace religion in its capacity to fill that spiritual urge, that compulsion to make sense of the world, to understand ourselves and become better people. Art can explain to us why love and kindness are what matters most, providing cathartic release. Open up the broken cup, let goodly sin and sunshine in. Drake or Coyne or, indeed, John Clare could have written those words.

Would they have liked each other's music? Doubtful, though their worldviews had much in common. Failure is a more universal experience than success. Both recognised this and wrote about it. Yet artists do require, at a bare minimum, just enough success to keep them going, to give them the self-confidence that makes creating that work possible. Kevin had that confidence much of the time. Nick Drake had it in the sixties but lost it in the early seventies. Both kept at it for as long as they felt able, which is the most any of us can do. Both will last.

GAFFA in 2022

For many years, Nottingham was not a live music city. There were no large venues. In the 1960s, big touring acts would play the Odeon Cinema and the church-like Albert Hall, often with multiple big name headliners, but by 1968 those days were over. The Playhouse and Theatre Royal weren't ideal for rock, though they occasionally had interesting acts. By the '70s, Lacemarket clubs like The Dungeon and The Beachcomber were long gone and the famous Boat Club (capacity 300) had long since passed its heyday.

I arrived in 1976. That autumn I saw Joan Armatrading and Oscar Peterson at the Albert Hall, but the university's Portland Building was by now the city's biggest regular venue. We didn't get many of the big punk or new wave acts. In the late '70s, you had to travel to Leicester, Sheffield or Derby for most tours. Rock City, the now legendary venue, which holds 2000, didn't open until late 1980. Two years later the 2,500 capacity Royal Concert Hall opened.

Nor did the city have many homegrown acts to write home about. Paper Lace had a number one with a song about the American Civil War in 1974. More significant was guitarist Alvin Lee, from Wollaton. His blues rock band, Ten Years After, were big between 1969 and '74. The most artistically and commercially successful late twentieth-century act to come from Nottingham were Tindersticks, although they've remained far from the mainstream. I often saw their lead singer, Stuart Staples, in the singles branch of the Market Street record shop, Selectadisc, in the late '80s, when the nascent band was called Asphalt Ribbons.

The biggest acts so far this century have been Jake Bugg and Sleaford Mods. I'm keen on Sleaford Mods, the bitter-sweet songs of Gallery 47 and electronic band, The Soundcarriers, whose lack of mainstream success is baffling. But, for me, Gaffa will always be *the* Nottingham Band.

When I returned to Nottingham in autumn '77, former *Liquorice* editor Malcolm was doing occasional live reviews for the *NME*. Earlier that year, he'd reviewed local band, Gaffa. "Infectious melodies that lock and burrow into the back of the head... potential hit singles." As luck would have it, Gaffa were playing a club called Katies during Freshers' week, supporting The Tom Robinson Band, whose first single had just come out.

Gaffa on stage at Katies, Beeston, in October 1977

Katies was in Beeston, the town that adjoins the university campus. I joined the *Liquorice* gang at the show, and was introduced to the lead singer of the support band. The main thing I recall about the gig is that the club kept playing '2-4-6-8 Motorway' on the PA beforehand, then Robinson played it at least four times during his set. Robinson, who wore a school blazer and tie, didn't have a big repertoire to draw on. The audience was full of record company people because the TRB was so hot. None of them seized on the support act, but my first impressions were more than favourable, and I wanted to hear more.

Gaffa had a residency in the big back room of a pub called The Imperial, on St James Street, just off Nottingham's Old Market Square. I went to see them there the following Tuesday, and the one after that. And the one after that.

I liked everything about Gaffa. I liked their humour and their Nottingham accents. Until then, as a student, I'd hardly encountered the notoriously idiosyncratic, impossible-to-mimic local accent. I liked Gaffa's irreverent, self-deprecating stage presence. I particularly liked Wayne Evans' lyrics, which were witty, often surreal but also laced with the kind of awkward truth bombs that had drawn me to Kevin Coyne. Wayne was good on adolescent angst, all those embarrassing areas that I would later be drawn to write about in my Young Adult fiction. Most of all, I liked Gaffa's music. They were a band of writers whose songs were catchy, varied in interesting ways and, more often than not, exciting.

Going to The Imperial every week, watching the Gaffa phenomenon in full flood, was invigorating. The band had just recorded their first EP, *Normal Service Will Never Be Resumed*, which would be the *NME*'s EP of the week and was noticed in *Sounds* and *Melody Maker* too. The EP, on Cleverly Records, compares favourably to Squeeze's much more generic debut EP, on Deptford Fun City Records. *Packet of Three* came out around the same time. Play the pair back to back and ask which band would still be making a good living forty-five years later. Not that any of us could imagine a band lasting so long.

One, otherwise favourable review called Gaffa 'Art School Clever Dicks'. Actually, only John Maslen, several years older than the others, had gone through Higher Education. He had a degree in History of Art and English Literature from Manchester University. Even then, during four years of study followed by a lecturing job in St Albans, he'd constantly played in bands.

Gaffa, while they might be working class lads, did have 'arty' tendencies. They used differing time signatures and complex song structures. Their modern equivalent would, perhaps, be the twenty-first century indie band Field Music, who write very catchy songs, but have unashamed prog rock elements and hate sticking to any formula for long. This has made them a hard commercial sell, much as Gaffa proved to be.

By the time I first saw them, Gaffa had a repertoire of about sixty original songs. Each week, it felt like, there'd be a new song or two. No covers, unless you counted a snatch of the *Fireball XL5* theme tune in Myph's doo-wop pastiche 'First Teenager on the Moon'. Gaffa weren't trying to emulate the Silver Beatles' marathon sets at Hamburg's Kaiserkeller. That

Gaffa at Wollaton Hall, 1978

said, the Imperial did have a bit of Liverpool's Cavern Club about it. Nobody danced. I usually got there in time to get a chair with my mates but there'd be lots of people standing, too, as well as those who sat cross-legged on the floor in front of the stage, which was mostly what people did when gigs took place on dancefloors. The big back room held 300 but was often over-sold. The queue would stretch down the street, sometimes round the corner into the square. Admittance was 50p.

Sounds gave Gaffa their second national music press review:

> OK, so the *NME* were the first to run a Gaffa live review, but that was close on three months before and then they only mentioned about Gaffa being the 'Nottingham' band. Let *Sounds* be the first to tell you that Gaffa are – plain and

simple – the band, full stop... a similarly keen eye for the lampoon, the parody and the collective tongue in the collective cheek style of song and performance of same... they stormed through a solid hour of highly original material and the cramped stage, consisting of merely a carpeted floor, appearing not to hinder the performance of the band one iota.

Gaffa's classic line-up took years to evolve. Wayne Evans met drummer Mick Barratt at The Imperial when they were seventeen or eighteen. He'd already seen Mick's first band, Hogweed, at The 360 club in Bulwell. Joined by Nick Turner and two other friends, they decided to form a new group. The friendship with Mick gave Wayne confidence to write. "We didn't want to be a covers band. Mick and I were very firm about that from the start..." Gaffa went through a number of guitarists before John Maslen was persuaded to join them: "We saw him peering out at us from under a straw cowboy hat at The Embankment at a Radio Nottingham gig." Guitarist Clive 'Myph' Smith came soon after and "it really started to gel."

Gaffa got going during the pub-rock era (1973-6). At one point they were lined up to support Roxy Music on a tour. "Then Roxy had a bit hit and they got Blackfoot Sue instead." They played quite a few London gigs but not enough to build a following there. Wayne: "London, in those days, it just seemed so far away. Especially in the vans we had."

The Imperial residency probably began around 1976 (memories are a little hazy). John, with atypical braggadacio, convinced the pub's manager that Gaffa could fill the big room if The Imperial dropped the current band on Tuesday nights. Just after the residency started, he found a bunch of crushed, sour grapes had been pushed through his letterbox by the band they'd displaced, Cisco. Soon, Gaffa were, as he'd predicted, packing the place.

In those early days, Gaffa had a keyboard player, Brendan Kidulis, who sang his own songs. Brendan was very good at hitting the phone and chasing gigs to keep the now professional band in work. He left before Gaffa recorded their first album.

I once pointed out to Wayne how important Nottingham was in his songs. "What I was trying to do was sing in my own voice, which these days – Arctic Monkeys, Sleaford Mods – is quite commonplace. Then, everybody was going down the highway..."

The Imperial residency built to a crescendo between 77-79. "We had a very fast turnover of songs... we did a lot of work in five years, writing-wise. Several new songs most weeks."

Like Kevin Coyne during the same period, like Elvis Costello, who was about to put together The Attractions, Gaffa were fecund with inventive songs. But Coyne and Costello were not as profligate with styles as Gaffa. Early on, Costello wrote songs as quirky and nostalgic as 'Hoover Factory'. In '78, though, revenge was his big lyrical motif, and served him well. He would go into country (as Gaffa did with 'Lucky Lighter', set during the Second World War) and write a sympathetic song about a lonely pensioner (compare 'Veronica' to Gaffa's 'O.A.P. Sightings') but not while he was starting out. Gaffa wanted to do lots of different things, and they wanted to do them all at once.

How to define an autobiographical song like 'Rotten Role Doormat' which was to close the first side of their first LP? It belongs to no genre. The autobiographical medley veers all over the place with screeching guitars, rock sections, a pointed 'art for art's sake' quip, hints of surf music. Impossible to categorise, yet Gaffa's songs were undeniably catchy. We all thought that, with the right production and promotion, they'd have hit singles.

I enjoyed my new joint honours course, which had a tiny cohort of nine or ten. I got on best with Chris from London. Introducing himself, he told me he'd spent his gap year "surfing the crest of the new wave." Punk and new wave had happened over the previous eighteen months, but Gaffa hadn't been assigned to either movement. Their main reaction to punk, John Maslen says, was to play a bit faster.

Chris and I read each other's poems. I still wanted to write about music, too. With *Liquorice* over, I began writing reviews for the student union fortnightly newspaper, *Gongster*. In January I became its music editor. By the third term I was co-editing the whole paper. Over the year, I ran two or three reviews of Gaffa, the second one illustrated by a photo of Wayne sniffing a coke bottle.

In February '78, after one of the Imperial shows, I interviewed Wayne at photographer Pete Coleman's house on Mount Hooton Terrace. The previous year, during my brief stint as an editor on *Liquorice*, I'd sat on Pete's stairs,

Wayne Evans emulates the stars.

GAFFA

"HELLO, Young Lovers," Valentine's day at the Imperial Hotel, Nottingham. "I've been waiting for this moment all week long"—Gaffa, just another local band, in their stage gear for their Tuesday night residency, right?

Wrong. Gaffa are, for my money, the most original, witty and entertaining group to have emerged in the last eighteen months, and what they are doing still struggling for a living in Nottingham is totally beyond me.

They open with all four songs from their soon to be re-released "Normal service will never be resumed" EP, stronger performances than on that record. "Married Man" is introduced, "This is what happens after Valentine's Day."

The set lasts over 90 minutes — all original material—an astonishingly large repertoire for such a new group. My only criticism actually, based on this, and their Tom Robinson support, is the set tends to lag a little in the middle—this may, of course, be partly due to my not knowing all the songs, but I reckon it could be a good idea for the band to do two short sets, instead of one long one.

Attempting to define Gaffa's music is difficult—stylistically they are very varied—ranging from surrogate Beach Boys to songs like "Paris," which approach hard rock. Their songs tend to involve a blanket irony, occasionally only implied, occasionally leaning towards sarcasm.

This isn't everybody's cup of tea —one young lady at the gig turned round half-way through and spat "Bloody Pseuds !"—one man's wit is another woman's proud, I suppose.

Gaffa obviously draw a large regular following though and, at their best their songs, as well as being catchy and original, are very funny, as in "The First Teenager on the Moon," when the lead guitarist puts on a space helmet and the band breaks the song to play the Fireball XL5" these (the original record of which, incidentally, was the first I ever bought, ah, nostalgia!) or their parody of the false ending gimmick.

Catch Gaffa while you can. If any kind of justice prevails in the music industry then it won't be long before they get a major record deal and have success of the same height as their critical acclaim.

I'm interviewing the group the night this issue comes out, and the result should be in our next issue.

DLB.

holding the phone so that Malcolm could make notes while he interviewed a pair of snotty youths from a new band called The Sex Pistols. We weren't to know that the tour they were touting would be mostly cancelled. Nor that punk would soon make *Liquorice* and the acts it championed seem much less relevant.

My interview, 'The Trials and Tribulations of Being the Gaffas' was published in *Gongster* on March 7th, 1978. I asked Wayne whether he was frustrated by their failure to be signed to a major label. "Perhaps it's fortunate in a way," Wayne said. "I've got a feeling that we've been saved. It's fate that it is gonna take time, and by that time I'm gonna be better. If I had a record contract a year ago I wouldn't be able to handle it as well as I could now."

The problem seemed to be that record companies didn't know where to place them. "What would they file us under? Progressive/Rock/Folk/Jazz?" They couldn't even get a John Peel session because producer John Walters thought that they were too 'arty.' He told them that they were trying 'too hard' to play their instruments. Wayne replied, "If the plumber comes to your house do you tell him to keep the tap dripping?"

Wayne, who would have been twenty-five at the time, told me that he'd been trying to pay his mother board since he left school, but he'd only managed it since last April. "It's a silly world, rock'n'roll. I'd like to get amongst it and drive holes into it. Mind you, thousands of people have thought that, but I think everybody can alter it a little bit: you owe it to yourself not to start doing the same old rubbish."

That was the end of the interview, but when I played the tape back in my student hall of residence, I found that Wayne had recorded a message at the end while I was using the loo. "Please can we have a gig at the university for £700 plus loads of grub afterwards, but don't let the drummer get any booze before we go on. Thank you."

Major labels came to see Gaffa in London, but no offer came. Never mind, this was the height of the 'do-it-yourself' era. Plans for a second EP, *Firm Favourites*, were ditched in favour of a full album. In the absence of a record company contract but with finance from John Barr, the band decided to record their first LP.

John Maslen's old friend Mike Finesilver was the owner of Pathway Studios (funded by income from his co-write of Arthur Brown's hit, 'Fire'), where Nick Lowe recorded many artists for Stiff Records. John had been in Pathway's house band after leaving university, while also teaching Liberal Arts at a college in St Alban's. Pathway was one of the cheapest studios in London. John worked with numerous different musicians there while developing his own style.

Gaffa's first EP was produced by Tim Humphries, the band's sound mixing maestro at The Imperial. After that, Mike Finesilver was to produce all of Gaffa's records, which would be released on Gaffa 'n' Products. The singles were all recorded at Pathway but the album was recorded at Berwick Studios in Soho. Gaffa had the day shift. At night the remaining original Sex Pistols (Steve Jones and Paul Cook, the pair *Liquorice* had interviewed two years earlier), along with sundry others, recorded the band's feeble swansong *The Great Rock'n'Roll Swindle*.

The Tuesday evening early in 1979 when Gaffa launched their first album, *Neither Use Nor Ornament*, felt momentous and celebratory. There was more sense of a Gaffa community that night than on any other I can recall. The band played every track in the order they appear on the record. Halfway through, Wayne mimed turning over the disc. At the end of the evening, I bought my copy, which is number fifteen. The album, which even had a double page insert collecting all the lyrics, looked great.

Neither Use Nor Ornament is a very Nottingham phrase that needs no unravelling. There's a copy of the album in John

Peel's archived record boxes. He must have played a track or two on Radio 1. Yet once I got my copy home, I had the same reaction as many Gaffa fans. Most of the songs we loved were there, but the album didn't quite work. The production was too dense. "It sounded too clean," Wayne told me when it was reissued in 2014. "People were used to hearing a buzzy sound through our sellotaped amps. But the remaster sounds great: there's a lot more space in it."

Listening to the LP on a good stereo, forty-four years later, the original verdict seems harsh on Mike Finesilver. Many well-received punk and new wave albums had much worse production. The 2014 CD remaster does make it sound a little punchier, more crisp. You can hear the remastered album, as well as the John Peel session that Gaffa did eventually record, in 1979, at https://soundcloud.com/gaffa-nottingham and judge for yourself. The LP is, I think, a fair representation of Gaffa as they were in 1978.

Too fair, perhaps. For Gaffa were many things. Half of *NUNO*'s fifteen songs, including 'Throw Me to the Christians', 'Go on then, Jump' and 'Baby Sitting' show the band in the witty rock meets pop mode that might be considered their commercial side. There's also a country song, two of John's more serious numbers ('Hollow City', 'Trackless') and one from Clive (the doo-wop pastiche 'First Teenager on the Moon', a live favourite, the one which interpolates the *Fireball XL5* theme). Even Mick gets a vocal, on the touching rap (long before rap) about becoming estranged from your mates, 'Some are in Suits (And Some are in Groups)', a number which has distinct soul elements. One can imagine reviewers asking "what kind of group have we here?"

Today *NUNO* sounds more like literate pub rock than punk rock. Perhaps it was too quirky for its own good. Why, there was even an ambivalent number about a white girl who likes reggae and gets called 'Black Meat'. Clear where the band's sympathy lay, but that one was never going to get played on the radio.

My life changed early in 1979 when I met Barbara, a third year medical student from Birmingham. I still got awkwardly self-conscious around women I liked. However, at my twenty-first birthday party, Mike, my oldest friend from Sheffield, treated us to a line of sulphate. The drug made me confident and loquacious. Mike introduced me to Barbara, who shared a house with an old schoolfriend of his, and we didn't part for the rest of the evening. Within a few months, she'd moved into the room next to mine in our student house.

I took Barbara to see Gaffa a few times, but no longer went every week. The group were still on course for success. They released two singles that year, both double A sides. The catchy, funny 'You Know I Love You (but I don't know how I know)' sounded like a hit when they played it live. Listening to the 7" today, the production is reminiscent of the commercially unsuccessful but influential Brinsley Schwarz (Nick Lowe's first band).

Splitting the 7"'s focus with John's more ambitious 'Hearts of Stone' (The Beat meet early XTC), while a touching act of band solidarity, probably didn't help promotion. The single came in a picture sleeve with a hand-painted lyric insert by John and his wife, Barbara Manuel. Each member of the band supplied a bespoke cover in the hope of attracting serious collectors to buy multiple copies, a technique that was to become popular in years to come. It is now Gaffa's hardest record to find.

Their next single, 'Attitude Dancing (Land of 1000 Dunces)' was more original. The tune, by Myph, has an interesting post-punk edge to it. That song tends to be regarded as the 'A' side. However, the other 'A' side of the single, 'Long Weekend,' is, for me, Gaffa's best song, It's complex yet catchy. With promotion and more FM-friendly production, its refrain could have made it a huge hit.

gaffa

you know i love you

(but i don't know how i know)

hearts of stone

a gaffa·n·product :: zzzz soo1

81

I never noticed before how many sad songs they play on
    the radio
Now you're not in our gang how many sad songs they play
    on the radio.

The song had a typically quirky Gaffa structure. Verse, verse, pre-chorus, chorus, instrumental break, middle eight, chorus, instrumental break, chorus, instrumental flourish finale. When I asked John Maslen how they'd come to structure it that way, he wrote back at length. John explained that the songs came from "Wayne's prose/poetry which mirrors perhaps the way immediate and more long-term perceptions are absorbed and flicker through his brain alongside other intellectual machinations permanently swirling around, collage-like, in his head." John identified the 'collage' aspect of bringing observations and opinion together that you find in Wayne's writing as a core aspect. "Wayne often writes whole songs with his own music and other times serves music supplied to him by sifting thru' his immense 'note pad' of scraps of paper on which he jots down overheard remarks, short poetic pieces or bits of things we send him... one of the first things I did when I joined Gaffa was to assist Wayne in getting his 'individual' way of writing into song structures."

The combination of John's long experience, which added breadth and depth of harmonic structure through his use of jazz chords, and Myph's steadily evolving, equally idiosyncratic approach gave Gaffa a unique style, one that was primarily designed to serve Wayne's songwriting. Wayne wrote 'Long Weekend' on his own, apart from the pre-chorus, for which Myph came up with the music. John

calls it a very good example of Wayne's application of 'movements' through to a song to suit what he's writing. The number also had a killer guitar refrain using Myph's signature surf sound.

Why was it not a hit? After all, during that era plenty of songs on tiny labels did at least scrape into the charts. Being a double A side can't have helped. Double A sides were never really equal (with the possible exception of The Beatles' 'Penny Lane'/'Strawberry Fields Forever'), so much as insurance policies. Record companies were hedging their bets. If one track didn't take off, the DJ might flip it (a good example of this is Rod Stewart's 'Reason to Believe'/'Maggie May').

Radio DJs tend to like songs about the radio. If the band had made 'Long Weekend' the only A side and retitled it 'Sad Songs on the Radio' it might have had a chance of being their breakthrough, despite the innovative structure. But 'Long Weekend' got lost. In time, the other 'A' side, 'Attitude Dancing' would have the widest reach of any Gaffa song, featuring on Bill Brewster's European post-punk and techno compilation *Tribal Rites* in 2017.

Forty years after the single's release, I was on BBC Radio Nottingham's equivalent of *Desert Island Discs* and chose 'Long Weekend' as one of my eight discs. My interviewer, veteran broadcaster John Holmes, brought in his copy of 'Attitude Dancing/Long Weekend' to show me. He was still a Gaffa fan, too.

There would be one more single, 'Man with a Motive', which came out in 1980. Jake Riviera paid for the recording. Gaffa, meanwhile, offered to pay back John Barr the money he'd given them for the LP. He wouldn't take it, so they used the money to press up the single, which featured Myph's most memorable Bondesque riff. I missed buying a copy at the time, maybe because I was skint after graduation, more likely because I didn't know it was out. I was in a sub-let, top floor flat on Wellington Square, looking down on the city centre, at work on the first of the two novels I attempted after graduating.

Gaffa's Imperial residency ended in 1980. The last time I saw them was at the Forest Recreation Ground, playing in the Rock and Reggae festival that took place every summer. They'd been persuaded by their producer to record a cover

Gaffa at the Rock and Reggae festival, Forest Recreation Ground, 1980

of the Lovin' Spoonful's 'Summer in the City' and performed it that afternoon. It was good. Then a disco cover beat them to the punch – this was the last significant year of disco – consequently their single wasn't released.

If living amongst the freaks in Colne hadn't already cured me of hippy tendencies, a visit to the Stonehenge Free Festival in 1980 completed the process. I was talked into going by Barbara. However this was a far cry from the Cambridge Folk Festival we'd camped at the year before. We hitchhiked all the way there, then slept through the solstice itself. Next day, we watched naked hippies dance between the standing stones and saw several bad bands. The experience was so dire, I didn't go to another rock festival for twenty years.

I did well in my finals but bad results from my bumpy second year dragged my degree result down. At the graduation ceremony, I neglected to remove my mortar board when I received my second-class degree, then managed to leave my degree certificate at the reception. I'd had a notion of doing a PhD on Irish literature while writing novels on the side, but my degree wasn't good enough to get a PhD grant.

I was aware of how few writers made a living. My daydream had been to get a novel published then land some part-time work in a university. Eventually, this would be how things panned out, but not for twenty-two years. That was when I started teaching a discipline – Creative Writing – that barely existed in 1980, at a university – Nottingham Trent – that didn't become a university until 1992.

In my Wellington Square flat, my autobiographical novel was soon abandoned for a more topical one. But, at twenty-three, I wasn't ready to start. I became politically active instead, giving talks about nuclear disarmament, which was a lot easier than writing my novel set in the aftermath of a nuclear attack. I was appointed a school governor and elected a Labour Party branch chair. I co-edited a journal called *Nottingham Labour Briefing* and considered going into politics. My skin, I soon worked out, wasn't thick enough, the Labour Party being as full of internecine struggles then as it is now.

Two of my next three years were spent on the dole, with a year on a job creation project in between, setting up a credit union for a housing society in the Lace Market. My bosses were fairly liberal – they weren't paying my salary, after all – and didn't seem to mind that I spent much of my time doing stuff for the Labour Party, N.U.P.E. (the union where I became a branch chair) and Nottingham for Nuclear Disarmament.

The credit union took in very little money but I still managed to mess up the accounts. During this period, Barbara and I moved into a hospital house together. The pressures of her unrelenting hours as a junior hospital doctor took their toll and we split up for the first, but not the last, time. We cared for each other too much to stay apart for long, but never fully got back together. Over the years we've managed to stay friends.

I found myself a cheap terraced house to rent on Forster Street, in the heart of Alan Sillitoe's Radford. When I had a bit of money, I haunted shops on the Alfreton Road that sold cheap second-hand vinyl and a bric-à-brac shop on Radford Boulevard that sometimes had green Penguin Ed McBains. These mysteries would become touchstones when I began writing crime novels. Occasionally, I wrote a little fiction.

I also stood for the city council, in the area where I now live, which was then a safe Tory seat. I didn't want a winnable seat because I didn't want to be a councillor. I had other plans. Ironically, 1983 turned out to be the last year in which the Tories won Nottingham, by one seat, yet Sherwood was the only ward in the city with a swing to Labour. Thankfully, the swing wasn't sufficient to see me elected.

By the time I met my partner, Sue, in autumn 1983, I was twenty-five and had returned to the University of Nottingham to train to be an English and Drama teacher. I'd had an offer from the journalism course which Sheffield Mike had taken. I turned that down, figuring that if I wrote for a living, I wouldn't be inclined to write fiction in my spare time.

The hippy in me had all but gone, as had the crippling, adolescent self-consciousness. A working-class Stevenage girl, Sue initially took against me. She found my forceful political opinions suspect. I'd yet to shake off the naïve arrogance of youth, although, without that, I might not have had the confidence to pursue a woman, who was, in every respect, out of my league. Still, we had a lot in common and never ran out of things to talk about. I hung in there, somehow seeing off several other suitors, and regrew my beard, which she liked. We were still a couple by the end of her year-long teacher training course.

I didn't apply for jobs until Sue got one because I was determined to follow her wherever she went. I remember the relief when she walked out of an interview down south because she didn't like the school's set-up. In 1984, the Nottingham jobs came up late, but she got the first one she applied for, in Radcliffe-on-Trent, and our lives, little though we knew it at the time, were determined. We would stay in this city and make it our permanent home.

Sue moved into Forster Street later that summer. Despite having no paid teaching experience, I managed to talk myself onto the city's supply register. Some school would be desperate enough to employ me, I figured, and was soon proved right. I worked in most of Nottingham's inner-city secondary schools, teaching any subject but my own. This rough initiation taught me more than I taught any of my students, not least that, for all my ideas about social justice, I'd be a much more effective teacher if I worked in a middle-class area.

The following Easter we bought a house in nearby Bobbers Mill. The same month I got an English teaching job at Rushcliffe Comprehensive in wealthy West Bridgford. This would be the only permanent, full-time job I ever had.

Over the next few years, while teaching full time, Sue and I supported each other's writing, neither of us resenting the investment of time that learning to write well requires. Her poetry was published much more quickly than my short stories. However, by the mid-'90s I was making a good living from Young Adult (YA) fiction, with my own crime series, Nottingham-based *The Beat*.

When Gaffa broke up in late 1980 there were no farewell shows. Founding member Mick Barratt was fed up of not making money, and who could blame him? He took a long holiday in California and they got in a substitute drummer. The States, he says, turned his head and he considered moving there. On his return to Nottingham, he quit the band, though he would play with Gaffa members on and off for the next twenty-three years.

Bands have a natural lifespan. Gaffa had given it a good go. But endings are rarely neat, especially in a tightly-knit music community like Nottingham's. John Maslen briefly took over on drums and they continued for a while as a three-piece. Then they tried out different drummers and Gaffa merged into a more casual grouping, The Florida Snowshifters, with Dawn Foxhall on vocals and Stevie Otter on drums. Then there was The Marcel Marceau Sound with Wayne and, latterly, Mick.

Wayne fronted a Cuban-influenced group called Mas Y Mas, for whom he played double bass. Since 2004, he's also played 'psycho country folk' in The Last Pedestrians. This band was fronted by his and Mick's old mate, Harry Stephenson, who had previously led Plummet Airlines, the one Nottingham band that did manage to release a single on Stiff ('Silver Shirt'/'This is the World' – it was not a hit). In between there was Harry and the Atoms, with Wayne and Myph, and The Loose Cannons, which also featured Mick.

Mick did get offered decent paying work. In 1980, a London band with a two-album deal and an American tour in six weeks' time urged him to join them. He's forgotten their name, but it was heavy rock in the Bad Company mode and "I told them I've never played music I don't enjoy." When Topper Headon was kicked out of The Clash in 1982, Mick was invited to audition. He took a train to London with Harry Stephenson. That evening, the pair got wasted on dope. In the morning, Mick couldn't be arsed to cross London for the audition.

After 1980, Wayne always managed to get by playing music. John Maslen stopped playing in bands in 1983, when he became a dad, working in education and, later, for the City

Council. Clive 'Myph' Smith did a degree in Heritage Studies at what is now Nottingham Trent University, then worked for the Open University until retirement. Mick Barratt worked as a fabric cutter in the '80s, then as a chef, before leaving Nottingham in 2003. Brendan Kidulis, their sometime keyboard player, moved abroad and is currently pianist and singer in residence at the Hotel Baltic in Zinnowitz on the German island of Usedom.

I've had three careers. Five years of full-time teaching were the hardest work I've ever done. I went part-time in 1990, just before my first novel, *The Foggiest*, came out. By 1994, I was making enough from my YA fiction to write full time. Since 2002 I've had a part-time Creative Writing lectureship at Nottingham Trent University, where I led the Creative Writing MA for several years and still teach two days a week. In 2011, when this story resumes, I'd just started writing about music in print for the first time since leaving university.

In 2000, encouraged by Sue's old university friend Mike Atkinson (henceforth, Nottingham Mike), I set up one of the first author blogs on the internet (at first on Geocities, since 2003 at www.davidbelbin.com) and often wrote about music on it: from a fan's point of view, not formal reviews. The most-read items on the blog have been my diaries of visits to the Glastonbury Festival. Twenty years after that awful Stonehenge experience, I'd gone to Glastonbury to research a YA novel, *Festival*, and enjoyed myself so much that I started going to Glastonbury, then the smaller Green Man in Wales, with increasing regularity.

Sheffield Mike and Nottingham Mike had each, meanwhile, become occasional rock critics, writing for Sheffield's *The Star* and the *Nottingham Post* respectively. The two Mikes were already the people I went to the most gigs with. Now I went to even more, as their guest, seeing lots of free shows in both cities.

In 2009, I was meant to be the plus one when Nottingham Mike was reviewing MGMT at Rock City. He had to pull out, but suggested I do it instead. Shortly afterwards, he couldn't make a gig by a new band called The XX at the Bodega Social, so I wrote about that too, for the *Nottingham Post*.

I started being sent the list of gigs available to review. Until the pandemic, I reviewed gigs most weeks, anyone from Georgie Fame to the Arctic Monkeys, with the occasional stand-up comedian. I gave the Sleaford Mods their first *Post* review when they supported Scritti Politti at the Rescue Rooms. Jason Williamson, I wrote, had the most authentic Nottingham voice since Wayne Evans of Gaffa. I'm not sure how many readers understood the reference.

On Christmas Day 2010, I had an email from John Maslen, who'd tracked me down via my website. John had returned to music in the '90s, forming his band Nth Degree, who'd gigged all over the UK and Ireland. He'd retired from the City Council at the turn of the century, but carried on doing writing work for an art and design company. His email read:

> myself, wayne evans and clive smith are recovering 18 'pertinent' gaffa songs from our back catalogue at the gallery on march 5 2011.

Gaffa were to reform for the first time in thirty years. They were doing a free gig in the big bar area of Nottingham Contemporary. The new art gallery had been carved into a sandstone cliff which once housed a Saxon fort. I asked Simon Wilson, the *Post* entertainment editor, to let me review the show, even though it wasn't on his list. Simon was too young to know much about Gaffa but took me on trust.

The gallery was a prestigious place to play. Hosting Gaffa was an astute move on the new building's part, establishing that the venue wanted to be part of Nottingham's history and communities, and wasn't just for the elite.

If there had been any doubt about Gaffa's enduring legacy in Nottingham, it was dispelled when I walked into Contemporary's big café-bar. The place was full of familiar faces, many of which I hadn't seen for decades. The crowd exceeded the three hundred who used to fill the back room of The Imperial. Old fans brought their kids. As in the Imperial days, there was a combination of cramped tables and standing, although the '70s tradition of sitting cross-legged for an entire show didn't return. A few numbers in, to a huge cheer, Wayne brought out his signature frog-shaped bass, a symbol that this was a band who never took themselves too seriously.

Many old favourites were played. Never-recorded songs like 'The Organic Shuffle', 'Disco Funeral' and, especially 'Parish' ('This city is where my friends are/this city is where I'm going to stay') held up well. The band even pulled out two unrehearsed encores that they used to play at The Imperial, country pastiche 'Lucky Lighter' and the even earlier 'Loon

Gaffa at Nottingham Contemporary

Pant £2.50 Blues'. "For those last few minutes," my review concluded, "it could be a Tuesday night in the big back room at The Imperial on St. James Street, back in the day."

The piece had one unexpected consequence. Guitarist Clive 'Myph' Smith had mentioned to me that he was about to become a grandad, not expecting that I'd use this detail in the review. Myph had to hurry round to see his mother before her evening paper arrived. He hadn't got round to telling her that she was going to be a great-grandmother.

The reunion led to the band meeting up again. A remastered CD issue of *Neither Use Nor Ornament* was released to accompany *XIXIIXIII*, an EP containing four new songs.

These felt modern, but remained, unmistakeably, by Gaffa. Opening track 'Rocking Science' sums up their concerns. 'I'm the man who stood next to the man who held the coats of the also-rans,' Wayne sings, only for the narrator to 'wind up playing stand-up bass in a party band.' The lyric refers to Cuban influenced Mas Y Mas. Their drummer Simon Bowhill and percussionist Richard Kensington completed the twenty-first century Gaffa line-up.

A second Contemporary show was arranged. This time, Simon agreed to run a feature in the *Post*. That was why, thirty-six years after I had first interviewed Gaffa's lead singer and lyricist, Wayne Evans, I interviewed him again. We began by talking about the time when the band were coming up with several new songs most weeks. Why didn't the band get picked up by a major?

"We were out there playing, but we had no management. Nobody was doing the follow-up business we should have been doing. We went to the end of the diving board, but pools weren't being made. Nowadays there's a great infrastructure for young bands in Nottingham, but we were doing it all ourselves.

"But by then we were pretty tired. We'd all been doing it full time. Mick wanted to get a proper job and be able to buy a new shirt… we carried on and kind of mutated."

They felt the big time could still be round the corner. But their moment had passed. Even so, "everybody in the band has continued playing. I think that's why we're able to revisit that material so well. John had his own band, Nth Degree,

Myph's been playing with a rockabilly band and with me, in various bands. I've carried on writing. We have started writing again, as Gaffa."

The last question I asked Wayne was "If the sixty-year-old Wayne could talk to the twenty-five-year-old who made this album, what would he say?"

"Don't take yourself so seriously," Wayne replied, "but keep going. Have a bit more self confidence. And get a manager!"

The interview was given a double page spread in the middle of the *Post*, accompanied by a piece on Jake Bugg from nearby Clifton. The young star was headlining Nottingham Arena for the first time. The band were delighted that they'd been given more space than him.

Would Gaffa have done better if they had, as Wayne suggested, had a good manager? Maybe, if they had found someone special who didn't try to change what made them unique. But what made the band so good, as with Kevin Coyne, also made it harder for them to reach a mass audience.

Financial success and fame can be the result of ruthless targeting of an audience, of sticking to a successful formula and sucking up to the right people. But success, like most things in life, is more often down to luck. Getting success and holding onto it isn't easy.

Around the turn of the century, the Harry Potter phenomenon considerably reduced the YA market. My children's fiction agent, Jenny Luithlen, found me new kinds of work and several new publishers, but my income halved.

Once I had the part-time university job, I was ready to move onto writing adult fiction. Soon, I was with one of the biggest agents in the business. She came tantalisingly close to selling my debut 'adult' novel, *The Pretender*, to a big publisher, but didn't succeed.

After two years, she dumped me because what I wanted to write next, a crime fiction sequence that followed the New Labour years, was unlikely to sell abroad. The sequence wouldn't make the agency enough money to justify their representing me.

I was lucky enough to get another agent, Al, who I'm still with, who placed *Bone and Cane* at a prestigious Birmingham press. Things started off well, with an Amazon Fiction number one. The second novel in the sequence got the good notice in *The Guardian* I'd always hankered after.

Soon, however, things fell apart. My publishers, Tindal Street Press, went bust before the mass market edition of the new book could be published.

The next one, you hope for a long while, will turn things round. But, in publishing, these days, you are only as good as the sales of your last book. One flop and you're done. The music business is equally ruthless. You're a winner, or you're nothing.

There was a brief Gaffa reunion in 2015, but it passed me by. My 2015 was a year of huge highs and lows. I chaired the company bidding for Nottingham to become a UNESCO City of Literature, which was – rather unexpectedly – successful. Chairing the NUCoL company dominated my working life until 2021. In between our bid's submission in July and the award in December, my oldest friend, Michael Russell (Sheffield Mike), died of cancer.

The last gig Mike and I went to together was a Libertines reunion at Rock City earlier in the year. Mike had never seen the original band and insisted on buying us tickets, even though he was too weak to walk far. At the back of the wildly moshing dance floor, I tried to shield him with my body. After a while he insisted on going off on his own and managed to watch the set from some stairs.

Mike was pleased and proud to have made it through the whole gig. Music meant the world to him. I wonder what he would have made of this book. He never saw Gaffa and couldn't stand Kevin Coyne, but did come round to Nick Drake. He'd probably tease me about all the embarrassing stuff I've left out.

I only caught up with Gaffa's 2015 album *Lift Us Up, and Leave Us There* recently. It's a good listen, more laid back than the band were in the '70s, less quirky but fun, with a frequent country feel and lyrics that couldn't be by anybody but Wayne Evans. It can be found on Spotify.

In 2017 I downloaded *Footnote*, a solo album by John Maslen I'd read about in Nottingham's free monthly culture magazine *LeftLion*.

John had also recorded with Colin Staples, a Nottingham blues legend from the '60s. In 2020, John guested on a new album, *Countless Branches*, from his old friend, singer/songwriter, Bill Fay, who had disappeared from music in 1971. Fay has been having a remarkable late career revival, of the kind I like to think might have happened to Nick Drake, had he lived.

The next time I heard about Gaffa was in between lockdowns in 2020. Pete Clark, who works in the box office at Nottingham's independent cinema, Broadway, had started playing drums with the band. Pete would update me from time to time, as did Clive (Myph) when I ran into him. There were never any firm gig plans, but they were recording. Pete was an improvisatory, inventive drummer, like Mick, which boded well for new Gaffa material.

In late 2021, Gaffa released an album, *Beaks and Bones for Buttons*, which can be heard at https://soundcloud.com/user-80645345/sets/beaks-and-bones-for-buttons. I've grown to like it a great deal.

Over eight songs, we're back in Wayne's wide-eyed, jaded yet surreal view of the world. The band's mature work doesn't have big hooks, but is distinctly Gaffa, with classy musicianship, interesting structures and crisp production. The musical style embraces anything from ragas to traditional folk (Myph's 'When Mary Gets Back From England'). Opener '(pricked up my ears when the) Beatles went Weird' pulled me in immediately. There's also the endearing wonky pop of 'Middle Distance' and the strange, spoken soliloquy that forms the title track. None of the songs could be by anybody else.

I wanted to see the new line-up live and broached the idea of their playing the launch of this book (which, at the time, consisted of the first two chapters). They were up for it. That was when I realised that the hybrid memoir I was writing would feel far more complete if I added a chapter about them. Gaffa were, after all, an indelible a part of my university years. Their connection with Nottingham was equally indelible. And I had already writtem more about them than I had any other musicians.

A couple of weeks later, I found out that Gaffa's original, classic line-up were to reform for a one-off show. Mick and Wayne had remained close friends, Wayne supporting Mick through cancer treatment a few years ago. In May, Mick had happened to come along to one of their rehearsals, played some bongos and enjoyed himself. The band were going to play at the Lincolnshire Poacher on Mansfield Road on Sunday, June 19th, 2022.

The new Gaffa album, *Beaks and Bones for Buttons*, had sleeve notes by former *Liquorice* editor Malcolm Heyhoe. We'd broken contact in the late '80s, a period when Malcolm got heavily into horse racing. I'd only bumped into him a couple of times since, at gigs, but knew he'd gone on to become a widely published racing correspondent. That Sunday night, when I arrived at the busy Poacher, he was the first person I recognised. I managed to get a stool near him, close to the corner stage.

Friendships can feel frozen in time. Talking to Malc again, part of me felt like the seventeen-year-old I was when I first met him. We discussed Gaffa and Kevin Coyne. I introduced him to a friend, explaining that, without Malcolm, the magazine and Nick Drake, I would never have come to this city.

Despite the reunion nature of the show, Gaffa's set was carefully balanced between old songs, recent songs and ones that nobody had heard before, much as their Imperial sets used to be. They opened with 'What is this an Advert for?' the nearest they come to blues.

The first set included two songs I remembered from the '70s, although they'd never recorded either, 'Words Fail Me' and 'We Used To'. The latter's ennui was given extra punch by being repeated 44 years after it was written. 'We don't do that any more, we don't do nothing any more.'

The set ended a little early due to issues with the borrowed drum kit, so the second half started with the song that should have been the first set closer, Imperial favourite, 'Trust the Driver.'

Then they were into a wonderful 'Beatles Went Weird'. Best of all, though, was the song of theirs I'd chosen to play on

the radio. I couldn't help myself: I videoed them performing 'Long Weekend' on my phone, big smile on my face throughout.

The biggest cheer of the evening came when Mick was announced. Wayne ad-libbed 'some are in suits and some are in groups' before singing the last chorus of traditional set-closer 'Throw me to the Christians'.

It was a thrilling evening.

Afterwards, Mick asked me how I thought he'd done. Taken aback by the earnest question, I said something like, "You were great, mate, of course." Only later did he tell me that it was the first gig he'd played in fifteen years.

Gaffa endure. This isn't the end of their story, or mine. It is where we're up to, forty-five years after I first saw them. They're still making music, with no expectations of any reward beyond the satisfaction of the act itself. I'm still writing, with much the same rationale. Writing, like music, is primarily a vocation. The most meaningful success is to keep going, to do what you need to do without compromise. The only success worth chasing is artistic success.

Gaffa did what they had to do. That's why I don't think top management would necessarily have given them the breakthrough they deserved. Having a top agent didn't help me. I wrote a lot of things that my agent(s) advised me against doing out of what felt like artistic necessity. I wrote the things I wanted to write and they all got published. That's enough. If you don't keep challenging yourself to try new things, you might be commercially successful, but you won't be satisfied with your work. Artists need just enough encouragement to keep them going. Any more than that is a distraction from the task-in-hand.

Creativity, I keep hearing, is the most potent panacea for mental health. Nick Drake's fate reminds us that art doesn't work as straightforwardly as that. Nick couldn't write or play when he was in the throes of depression. Writing has helped my mental health and the same, I know from talking to them, goes for many of my peers. Writing is a place where you can mention the night, tackle your dark thoughts head on, and, sometimes, come to terms with them.

Looking back on my late teens has, at times, been excruciating. Most people learn to park their adolescent experiences, relieved they're long gone, but I keep being drawn back to mine. I feel a need to reconcile my adolescent self with my adult one. It seems like a healthy thing to do. I'm aware that many of my 'adult' (as against YA) novels, from *The Pretender* to the one I plan to write next, are about young men and women in the zone between adolescence and adulthood. It's a time when we're still learning, still shaping our view of the world.

But so much is down to chance. I've had my share of luck, more than my share. The artists discussed above were all lucky finds that I wouldn't have made in another time, another place. Each of them influenced the person I became. Being born in the West with free higher education and benefits sufficient to live on were also part of the luck I've thrived on. That luck is denied to most in today's UK, where a career in The Arts is increasingly the preserve of the already rich and privileged.

Enjoying art, and creating it, at any level, can make life worth living. I keep on keeping on with my writing for the same reason that Gaffa still make music: the process of making art is challenging, interesting, frequently fulfilling and occasionally, if you're lucky, exciting. It's an end in itself. Art for Art's sake. Ripe fruit in the tree. Dynamite, dynamite days...

Acknowledgements

The author would like to thank Gabrielle Drake and Cally Calloman, Richard Morton Jack, Eugene Coyne, Lesley Fox, Wayne Evans, Clive Smith, John Maslen, Mick Barratt, Pete Clark, Clive Product, Uwe Schillhabel, Paddy Stamp, Sue Dymoke and the book's dedicatee for their help and assorted permissions. Finally, thanks to Ross Bradshaw, without whom this accidental memoir wouldn't have been a flicker in my mind's eye.

Website: www.davidbelbin.com
Twitter: @dbelbin

Clive 'Myph' Smith, John Maslen, David Belbin, Mick Barrett and Wayne Eva
in the back yard of The Lincolnshire Poacher, June 19th, 2022